PRAISE FOR FIONA VALPY

'Fiona Valpy has an exquisite talent for creating characters so rounded and delightful that they almost feel like family, and this makes what happens to them feel very personal.'

—Louise Douglas, bestselling author of *The House by the Sea*

'A novel that will whisk you to another time and place, *The Storyteller of Casablanca* is a tender tale of hope, resilience, and new beginnings.'

—Imogen Clark, bestselling author of *Postcards From a Stranger*

'Love, love, loved it . . . Brilliant story, I was completely immersed in it, so moving and touching too. The research needed must have been hard to do but it brought the war . . . to life.'

—Lesley Pearse, author of *You'll Never See Me Again*

'A wonderfully immersive novel set against a vivid and beautifully described . . . setting. I loved it!'

—Victoria Connelly, bestselling author of *The Rose Girls*

'A moreish story of love, war, loss, and finding love again, set against an atmospheric . . . backdrop.'

—Gill Paul, author of *The Second Marriage*

T0061936

Light
Through
the Vines

OTHER TITLES BY FIONA VALPY:

The Storyteller of Casablanca

The Skylark's Secret

The Dressmaker's Gift

The Beekeeper's Promise

Sea of Memories

The Season of Dreams (previously published as *The French for Always*)

The Recipe for Hope (previously published as *The French for Christmas*)

Light Through *the* Vines

Fiona Valpy

LAKE UNION
PUBLISHING

Text copyright © 2013, 2022 by Fiona Valpy
All rights reserved.

Published by Lake Union Publishing, Seattle

First published as *The French for Love* by Bookouture in 2013. This edition contains editorial reversions.

www.apub.com

ISBN-13: 9781662503733
ISBN-10: 1662503733

Cover design by Emma Rogers

Printed in the United States of America

love : *vtr. aimer; affectionner;*
ressentir une attirance pour;
être amoureux; adorer; désirer;
faire l'amour;
n. amour m;
attirance passionnée f;
affection f;
tendresse f;
intérêt; personne aimée f;
mon chou, chéri, amour . . . ;
to fall in love : *tomber amoureux/amoureuse ;*
the love of his life : *l'amour de sa vie ;*
love at first sight : *le coup de foudre m;*
love affair : *liaison f; histoire d'amour f . . .*

Chapter 1

Admitting defeat, I give up on my attempts to do Pilates in a ferry cabin the size of a sardine tin – the first item on my daily to-do list. So much for the healthy resolution I made in the wake of Ed's departure. Instead, I go up on deck to stretch my legs and watch Saint-Malo materialise through the early morning mist. I take deep breaths of sea air as I stride the length of the ship, clearing my head for the day's drive ahead.

I scarcely slept last night, cocooned in my bunk as the ferry rocked and rolled its way across the Channel. Thoughts of Ed churned in my head, the waves of humiliation crashing over me again. Ed and Camilla. The woman he's been having an affair with. For several months, it turns out. And has now moved in with. Seamlessly, having packed his bags and moved out of my flat last week. Six days ago. And six lonely, sleepless nights, each of which has stretched itself out into a gaping chasm of minutes and seconds. Thank goodness I had this buying trip to France lined up. It's a more than welcome distraction.

I complete a second length of the deck and as we glide through the entrance to the harbour, the cries of the seagulls announce our arrival. Picking up my bags, I follow the tide of passengers back into the depths of the ship, making for the car deck.

◆ ◆ ◆

'I love my job,' I sing to myself. The radio's tuned to a French pop station that plays music so bad it's good, as I swing on to the autoroute and head south. I'm a buyer for an independent wine merchant called Wainright's, which has a handful of shops dotted across small towns in Sussex and Hampshire. I come to France a couple of times a year to visit producers and try any new wines that sound promising. It may sound quite glamorous, but the reality's a good deal more mundane. Most of my working hours are spent sitting behind my computer in the small, dusty office above the shop in Arundel. Once a month, I visit each of the shops to keep our staff up to date with the latest wine news and to help run tastings for clients. But the highlights are my twice-yearly hops across the Channel, visiting the wine regions. This time, I'm heading for the Loire and then on to Bordeaux. And I've tacked on a few days' holiday at the end, to stay with my favourite aunt.

Actually, she's my only aunt, but she'd have been my favourite even if I'd had others. She was quite well known, once upon a time. Liz Chamberlain became something of a celebrity in the swinging sixties, when she made a name for herself with her photography. Her iconic portraits of rock stars and artists are still reprinted occasionally (these days mainly accompanying obituaries). But she moved to the depths of rural France at the end of the seventies and completely turned her back on the glamour and buzz of her London life, becoming a bit of a recluse. She never lost her eye for beauty, although she turned her camera lens from celebrities to the countryside surrounding her new home, picking up commissions to take photos for books on the wines of Bordeaux and the landscapes and wildlife of southern France. Her passion has waned with the advent of digital photography as, she says, the challenge and artistry have gone now. 'It's the end of an era.'

I can't wait to see her. A few days spent sitting in her beautiful garden are just the therapy I need right now. I know she'll ask me all about the break-up with Ed and be outraged on my behalf. A good female solidarity session will give my battered self-esteem a much-needed boost, and Liz's dry wit and easy warmth are always balm for a bruised soul.

The flat northern landscape rolls by and a sign announces that I'm entering Picardie. The radio plays songs from years ago and I feel my spirits lift a little. It's been a tough twelve months and I admit I've struggled at times. The sledgehammer blow of Ed's betrayal and departure are nothing in comparison with Dad's death last year, which was more like being hit by a wrecking ball. What a double whammy: the break-up struck the open wound of my grief right on the spot. The pain in my heart feels utterly unbearable at times.

My father died much as he had lived, in a quiet, gentlemanly, considerate manner, falling silently to the ground in the back garden of my parents' home in West Sussex. It was a massive heart attack, the doctors explained. Out of the blue. Nothing anyone could have done. My mother was her usual poised self when she rang to tell me, and her cool, remote manner made me wonder – not for the first time – how much she had really loved my father. Sometimes it's hard to believe she and Liz are sisters, the one so warm, funny and bohemian, living her rather hermit-like life tucked away in the depths of rural France, and the other such a reserved and proper Sussex matron, with a penchant for social bridge and designer handbags.

We scattered Dad's ashes at the edge of the garden, where our boundary gives on to neighbouring fields and the view across to the rolling slopes of the South Downs, beside the bench where he used to come and sit. I'd sometimes find him there on summer evenings, watching the sky turning from blue to rose to black, as the swallows swooped and flitted overhead.

I blink to clear the pooling tears from my eyes and mentally give myself a little shake. Time to pull up at a service station for a croissant and a cup of strong black coffee. After my sleepless night and the early start this morning, I badly need a restorative boost of carbs and caffeine for the long drive ahead.

Chapter 2

After a week's foraging in the Loire, notching up hundreds of miles in my selfless quest for delicious wines, I arrive in Blaye, the most northerly point of the Bordeaux region. While the Loire Valley is a gracious and imposing region of France, with its air of refinement in both the area and the wines that are a source of quiet pride for its inhabitants, of the two regions I'm visiting on this trip, Bordeaux is my favourite.

The Loire has a dreamy quality to its elegant châteaux and their manicured grounds, while Bordeaux has a more gutsy, busy, purposeful feel. In the Médoc, the best known – and frighteningly expensive – *premier cru* châteaux make their prestigious wines, sought after the world over. Further east, the land rises into the clay and limestone ridges where you find Pomerol and Saint Émilion – journey's end for many a wine pilgrim. But these famous names tell only half the story. The region is rich in smaller châteaux that form the engine room of this powerhouse of world winemaking.

My boss, Harry Wainright, still handles the buying of *en primeur* from the *grands châteaux* but I come to dig and delve in the less well-known corners of the Bordeaux region to seek out the unknown but still excellent wines, the kind that sell for the sort of prices normal people pay.

After another day in the car, tonight I'm staying in a once gracious château that offers *chambres d'hôtes*. The owner, an effortlessly chic Frenchwoman, greets me and shows me to my room. Tall shuttered windows look out across the parkland at the front of the house, studded with magnificent chestnut trees whose tender green leaves are just beginning to unfurl.

The room is as elegant as its owner. Its high corniced ceiling gives it an airiness, despite the plethora of heavy pieces of antique furniture. The polished wooden floorboards and fine yet worn rugs are bathed in pools of light from the setting sun.

Before I walk into the village for supper at a small restaurant there, I reach for my notebook and lie on the bed, crossing items off my to-do list and reading through the notes I've made on the vineyards I'll be visiting in the next few days. Two are regular suppliers already, so these are really just courtesy calls to maintain contact and ensure the latest vintages are up to scratch. But I'll also visit a handful of other winemakers to research possible new lines. I jot down a couple of ideas for inclusion in the tasting notes I'll be compiling later and then, suddenly hungry, I pick up my handbag and jacket and hurry down the imposing staircase of the château, letting myself out of the heavy front door and closing it carefully behind me.

As I walk the few hundred yards along the small country lane into the village, I'm overcome with a longing to have my father here with me to share my solitary evening meal.

It was from Dad that I learned to taste wine. He made his living as a wine writer and became editor of a wine magazine, so wine was always a feature on the dinner table in our house. From an early age, he encouraged me to think about what I was tasting, in tiny quantities to be swirled around the mouth before spitting into a *crachoir*. One of my childhood delights was to watch him send a perfectly aimed stream of wine into the spittoon with a nonchalant elegance that completely belied the crudeness of the action, elevating it to a performance art.

He made me think about the different layers of flavour in each wine and encouraged me to describe what I could taste. 'Don't be shy,' he'd say. 'There's no right and wrong. It's a personal thing. Do you like it or not? If so, why? If not, why not?' He'd bring a handful of small jars from the spice rack in the kitchen and hold each one under my nose. 'Think about what you can smell. That's cinnamon, remember it. And this one that smells like sweaty socks is cumin – you'll often find a whiff of it in some of the very best wines. Along with just a hint of horse manure.' I'd giggle at the thought of sweaty socks and horse manure and Mum would tut disapprovingly.

But that education had led, eventually, to my job at Wainright's, starting out as a sales assistant, working hard and earning my promotions to shop manager, buying assistant and finally, two years ago, to buyer in my own right.

After an excellent meal in the local bistro, I pick my way back to the château somewhat gingerly. The night is as black as pitch on the small country road, but the sky is clear and the moon and stars light the way. I imagine my dad is walking with me, his presence as calm and comforting as ever, seeing me safely back to the château.

◆ ◆ ◆

At the end of a happy week foraging for wines, I finish up in the easternmost corner of the Bordeaux region, where Liz's rambling stone farmhouse perches on the edge of a ridge above the broad Dordogne valley.

The land surrounding the house, planted with plum orchards and neat rows of vines, was sold off long ago to local farmers. Liz bought just the house and its garden, a stretch of rough lawn bounded by tall oak trees. I turn into the lane between the vines and then up the dusty driveway. It's been a long couple of weeks on the road and I bring the car thankfully to a halt in her courtyard, where pots of blue grape hyacinths and creamy narcissus are in bloom. Later, in the summer, she'll plant out the bright geraniums that I know will be clustered on every windowsill in the house to keep them safe from the late frosts. The walls of the house, which form a right angle framing two sides of the yard, are built from the cream-coloured limestone that's part of the bedrock here, the same rock that the vines push their roots into, searching out the nutrients that help give the local wines their distinctive minerality and structure. The doors and windows, framed with wooden shutters, are painted the claret colour that is traditional about these parts, harmonising with the red roof tiles of the house. Liz's home seems to be opening its arms in an embrace, welcoming me.

Suddenly, I realise how exhausted I am, and how thankful to be here at last. It's not only the driving; speaking French is hard work too. I'm pretty good at the technicalities of winemaking, but normal, everyday, conversational French is still hard work. I'll be chatting away fairly fluently and then an unknown phrase will loom like a linguistic brick wall and I'll have to resort to miming or searching for the translation on my phone. It's definitely a relief to be back in English-speaking territory now my busy fortnight is over.

As I clamber out of the car, the kitchen door is flung open and Liz emerges, arms outstretched. 'Gina, darling,' she exclaims. 'You look as though you need a good meal and an even better night's sleep.'

I hug my aunt warmly. And am struck by a sudden feeling of frailty about her. She's always had a slim frame, it goes with her quick, busy energy, but I haven't seen her for almost a year and she's looking fragile, more bird-like than ever with her bright glance and neat cap of cropped white hair.

She ushers me into the kitchen. 'Come and meet my lovely neighbour. Mireille Thibault, my niece, Gina Peplow. I don't think you've met before?'

A tiny, very upright lady dressed in black shakes my hand, her face an etching of deep wrinkles that crease even further with her warm smile. 'Liz has told me a great deal about you,' she says in French, with just a slight twang of the *Sud-Ouest* accent that's common around here.

'Mireille lives in the house up the lane,' says Liz. I nod, having noticed the small stone cottage set among plum trees on walks with my aunt to forage for mushrooms or gather blackberries from the thickets of brambles that sprout exuberantly along the verge here and there.

'Yes, and now I must be getting back,' she smiles. 'Two of my grandchildren will be arriving any minute and if I don't get there first, they'll eat the whole of the cake I've made. They're always starving when they come out of school. Goodbye, Mademoiselle Gina. Enjoy your stay with your aunt.' She hugs Liz and disappears up the drive.

'What a nice woman,' I remark.

'Isn't she great?' says Liz. 'I'm lucky she bought the house along the lane and now I have such a good friend and neighbour. She lived closer to Sainte-Foy before that and moved here about a year ago after her husband died. Now,' she continues, holding me at arm's length to take a better look at me. 'What's first? I think a shower and unpack and then a nice glass of chilled wine? You look exhausted.'

I go out to the courtyard to bring my bags from the car, and as I re-enter the kitchen a large black cat appears, winding himself around my ankles.

'Hello, Lafite,' I say, putting my bag down and stooping to stroke his glossy coat. 'You're looking extremely well.' His deep purr reverberates in his chest, and he butts his broad head lovingly against my hand.

My aunt found a cat and two small kittens in her woodshed one early summer's day about a dozen years ago. No one in the area had any idea where they came from, although they weren't feral so Liz suspected they'd just been dumped with the unwelcome arrival of the two new additions. So she adopted them, naming the mother cat Margaux and the kittens Latour and Lafite. Sadly, Latour came to an early end when he ate some poison put down by a local farmer to kill foxes, but Margaux lived to a ripe old age and her remaining son is still going strong. 'How old is Lafite now?' I ask.

'He'll be thirteen in a couple of months' time. He's getting rather staid these days. Not nearly as good a mouser as he once was. He doesn't exactly earn his keep. Spends most of the time lying by the fire or on his chair in my bedroom. Still, he's good company.'

'And no doubt just as utterly pampered and adored as ever,' I say, with a laugh.

Liz shows me to the guest bedroom. Not that I need to be shown the way – it's thoroughly familiar from my many stays with her over the years.

In my teens, I started coming here on my own for a week or two during the summer holidays. First, Mum, Dad and I would have our family fortnight in Salcombe in July. My mother would lounge elegantly on the beach behind a large pair of sunglasses and the latest copy of *Tatler* or *Homes and Gardens*, while Dad and I made sandcastles. When I was old enough, he and I would sail a small dinghy upriver, away from the frenetic bustle of boats in the harbour, to explore the creeks hidden behind sloping shoulders of farmland. He'd always bring a pair of binoculars for bird-spotting. Once we saw a kingfisher, the colour and speed of an electric shock, dart down from a dead branch overhanging the water. And another time we sat side by side on the bank, entranced by the bizarre movements of a dipper as it bobbed and bowed on a rock before walking right into the water, foraging beneath the surface in search of food.

Then, with August still stretching before me, I'd be put on a plane and met at Bordeaux airport by Liz. My mother never seemed keen to come along – too much to do in the garden after being away in Devon, she said, and she'd miss her bridge. Secretly, I was pleased. My holidays with Liz were always wonderful, sun-drenched, fascinating weeks of freedom, helping her in her gloriously wild garden or visiting local markets to pick out fresh produce. We'd bring the food back so she could teach me to cook classic French dishes. She'd always choose a local wine to go with what we'd made, helping me understand how the right wine complements and enhances even the simplest meal.

I'm pleased to see that nothing in the spare room has been changed since last time I was here. The whitewashed walls are hung with framed photos of the local landscape. Liz's work, of course. I know and love each one: the stick-like vines on the *côteau* plunging into mist lying in the river valley below, which is rosy pink in the winter sunshine; the white clouds of blossom in the plum orchards in spring; a golden willow, perfectly reflected in hazy autumn light on the Dordogne. There are rag rugs on the terracotta tiled floor and a pretty *toile de Jouy* quilted spread on the double bed. I used to think it was the height of sophistication when I was younger, to sleep in such a big bed, quite unlike the modest one in my bedroom back at home. There's a jug of spring flowers on the bedside table, along with a small pile of paperbacks. Liz is an avid reader and I know she'll have put these to one side for me, thinking I'd enjoy them too.

'What bliss to be here again,' I say, turning to give her a hug.

'Make yourself at home and come down when you're ready,' she says, and kisses my forehead gently in return.

I settle myself in, setting my notebook next to the jug of flowers, hanging my work jackets in the wardrobe and unpacking clothes creased from weeks on the road.

When I come through to the kitchen half an hour later, a delicious smell greets me, and Liz, pushing a casserole back into the oven, straightens up from shutting the door. '*Coq au vin*,' she says. 'Hope that's okay.' She knows it's one of my favourites. Her recipe is the perfect comfort food, the syrupy juices suffused with earthy flavours of wild mushrooms and fragrant thyme. 'Now' – she turns to the fridge – 'where's that bottle of wine? Shall we take our glasses out to the terrace? The sun's going down but let's catch the last half hour of light.'

The terrace is on the west of the house, the other side from the courtyard. Even though it's still only early March there's warmth in the suntrap of its stone paving against the wall of the house. We settle ourselves on a bench, facing the setting sun.

As we watch, a magpie flutters down from the branches of an oak tree on to the grass, almost immediately followed by a second one. 'Two for joy,' I say. 'Very apt at this precise moment. You taught me that rhyme. How does it go? One for sorrow, two for joy, three for a girl, four for a boy. Five for silver, six for gold . . . And I forget what seven is?'

Liz smiles. 'Ah, seven. Seven for a secret never to be told. All of life is there really, in that one simple rhyme.' She takes a sip of her wine, musing for a moment. 'Clever birds, magpies. But they can be cruel and ruthless too. Which reminds me,' she says, eyebrows raised in an expression of mock innocence, 'how *is* Ed these days?'

'Aunt Elizabeth, really!' I protest feebly, my heart not in it, as she well knows.

'Well, what a bastard he is, carrying on behind your back like that. I hate to say it, but I didn't really take to him that time you brought him here last year. Too smooth for his own good. And not nearly good enough for you, if you ask me. Although, of course, you didn't and I'd never have dreamed of saying so at the time. And what was all that nonsense about the family name?' she continues, warming to her theme, comfortingly outraged on my behalf. 'A load of pompous rubbish.'

'I know,' I sigh. 'Edmund Wilberforce Cavendish. He was named after a bachelor uncle in the hope that he'd inherit some huge family pile. The funny thing is, though, the old bloke ended up marrying some glamorous divorcee at the eleventh hour. She had three children and he left the whole lot to them instead. So Ed ended up with nothing.'

'Well, it serves him right,' retorts Liz, still briskly indignant. She pauses, then says, a little more gently, 'Did you really love him?'

I hesitate, contemplating how to answer her question. 'I don't know if it was love exactly, but I'd become very used to having him around. It certainly wasn't a grand passion, but you can't hang around forever waiting for the love of your life to come along, you know. I did think we were probably going to get married eventually . . .' I tail off, hearing how half-hearted that sounds.

My good friend and fellow wine buyer at Wainright's, Annie Mackenzie, has a theory that the difference between good wine and mediocre wine is the same as the difference between good sex and mediocre sex: to be good, it has to engage the mind as well as the senses. Talking to Liz on that warm spring evening, Annie's theory pops into my mind and it suddenly strikes me that Ed has been more a bottle of plonk than a *grand cru*. More plonker than prince, now I come to think of it.

'Well, you deserve far better than that,' Liz retorts. 'The love of your life is exactly what you should be waiting for. Don't settle for anything less.'

'But what if the right man doesn't come along? What if I don't meet anyone?'

'Then you will live a happy and fulfilled life on your own,' Liz says firmly. 'It's not that bad, you know.'

'Is that what you did? Decide not to settle for anything less than the man of your dreams, I mean? Did he just never come along?'

Liz reaches down to deadhead some daffodils growing in a pot beside us. It's a nonchalant gesture, but it strikes me as maybe just a little self-conscious too, like she's avoiding meeting my eye.

'Oh, I met the man of my dreams all right. But it was complicated. In fact, so complicated that it was impossible. And yes, after that I did decide that I could never settle for second best. But that's way back in the past now.' From her brisk change of tone I know she's firmly fending off any further questions, so I resist the urge to ask them. 'It's far too late for an old dinosaur like me,' she continues. 'But you are a mere spring chicken, with everything going for you and time still on your side, so just hang on in there. What are you now? Twenty-eight?'

'Twenty-nine and counting.'

'Well, you're young. I know the right man for you will come along. And, anyway, you have your career as well, of course. How long have you been at Wainright's now? Must be getting on for ten years, isn't it? Do you think you might want to make a move at some stage?'

'I don't know.' I frown and take another sip of my wine. 'I love what I do – and I was perfectly happy to keep jogging along until recently. I suppose because I thought Ed and I might be starting a family before too long. Under those circumstances, I'd have been content just ticking over at work. Easier to balance the whole motherhood thing too. But now all that's changed, of course.'

'Ah, the eternal compromise of the working mother,' says Liz sagely. 'In my day you had to choose, but these days I thought you

14

could have it all – the fulfilling career and the clutch of perfect children too.'

'Hmm, I suspect the reality is still a little trickier, whatever it may look like on the pages of the glossy magazines. Anyway, I now appear to have neither.'

'Well, there's nothing to stop you applying for other jobs, is there? Any prospect of a promotion at Wainright's?'

'Only if Harry throws in the towel. As a France specialist, I'd need to go for his job. But sales aren't great right now, so it's probably safer for me to stay put.'

Liz laughs. 'Since when has safety been a consideration? Surely the time for you to take a few risks is now? In case you hadn't noticed, there's a big wide world out here, Gina, beyond the walls of your office above the shop back home.' She waves her glass towards the vines, startling the pair of magpies, who flutter off into the trees.

We sit in silence for a while, watching as the sun sinks lower and begins to paint the edges of the clouds in shades of rose and crimson. The air grows cold suddenly, and I notice Liz give a little shiver.

'Come on,' I say, picking up our empty glasses. 'Let's go inside and eat that delicious-smelling dinner you've cooked.'

I take her arm as we go and am struck once more at how terribly thin and frail it seems against my own.

◆ ◆ ◆

I sleep well that night and oh, the relief to wake up and see the hands of my watch standing at half past seven rather than two or three in the morning. I'd forgotten to close the shutters when I went to bed and the light is already streaming in, casting the fat buds on the wisteria branches hanging around the window into dancing shadows across the bedspread. I stretch, luxuriating in the knowledge of a good night's sleep behind me and a sunny day ahead. I can already hear Liz in the kitchen below, talking to Lafite as she puts food in his bowl. There's no great hurry to get up, and nothing to put on today's to-do list, so I look through the books beside my bed, select one from the pile and read for a while. Lafite, his breakfast devoured, shoulders open the door of my room with an enquiring chirrup and jumps on to the bed, settling down companionably beside me.

Once I'm finally up and dressed, I find Liz in her study. The book-lined room, with its tall, large-paned windows looking out on to the courtyard, is usually a comfortable muddle of papers, magazines and folders full of old photographs, negatives and contact sheets. But today it's even messier than ever, positively awash with heaps of paper in a kaleidoscope of colours and forms – and in the middle of it all sits my aunt, glasses perched on the end of her nose, peering at a folder of photos. I wade through the detritus and bend down to kiss her soft, wrinkled cheek.

She looks up with a slight start. 'Sorry, didn't see you there. I was back in the sixties with Mick and Ron.' She holds up a black-and-white print of the Rolling Stones grinning into the camera, fresh-faced versions of their current-day selves. 'I'm having a bit of a clear-out,' she explains with a sweep of her hand. 'Time I got rid of some of this nonsense. Which reminds me,' she continues, 'come upstairs to my room. I've got a few things I thought you might quite like.'

The bedroom takes up the entire attic of one wing of the long, low farmhouse. Liz converted it to living space when she first moved in, adding low windows beneath the eaves and skylights to let in the sun. The clear-out she's been having obviously extends to her wardrobe as well as her study. Piles of clothes are heaped across the floor and on every chair around the room. On the bed, next to a roll of black bin bags, there's a small pile, neatly folded. Liz picks up the top item and shakes it out, holding it up against herself. It's a top made of floating layers of creamy silk with long, softly flared sleeves and a plunging neckline.

'Wow, that's gorgeous!' I exclaim.

Liz hands it to me. 'Try it on and see if it fits. I thought it would suit you. It's an early Ossie Clark piece. Have a look through these others as well, see if there's anything else there you'd like. Here, take them to your room.' She puts the pile of rainbow-coloured fabrics into my arms and drapes the cream tunic across the top. 'You can try them on while I get your breakfast. Oh, and I meant to tell you, we're invited to Hugh and Celia Everett's for drinks this evening. You don't have to come if you don't want to, but they said you'd be most welcome.'

'I'd love to,' I reply. 'I'm very fond of them both.'

The Everetts are two of Liz's oldest friends. Celia was at school with my mother and my aunt, and she was head girl when Liz was a hippy rebel, according to my mother. Three years younger than the pair of them, Mum worshipped them both from the lowly ranks of the upper fourth. Despite their divergent styles, Liz and Celia remained friends and, having holidayed in the region for years, on Hugh's retirement from the Diplomatic Service, the Everetts bought a house a few miles from Liz and set about establishing themselves as linchpins of the local social scene.

'Well, there's sure to be a crowd there. Celia always invites the world and his wife. Perhaps there'll be an eligible bachelor we can team you up with,' Liz adds with an arch twinkle.

I grin and shake my head as I carry my spoils back to my room. She never misses a trick, that aunt of mine.

◆ ◆ ◆

As we arrive at the Everetts', Hugh throws open the door of their rather grand home on the outskirts of the picturesque village of Gensac and warmly embraces Liz, then turns to kiss me on both cheeks. 'Goodness me,' he says chivalrously, 'Gina, you just get more and more beautiful.'

I put it down to the vintage top Liz gave me. The minute I put it on, its clever, flattering cut draped softly and sexily over my figure and my complexion glowed against its soft colour. When I looked at my reflexion in the age-spotted wardrobe mirror in my room, I felt a sudden boost to my battered self-confidence. I've smudged concealer over the dark half-moons under my eyes, the tell-tale signs of my newly acquired insomniac status, and brushed a little blusher over my cheeks, camouflage to help get me through the evening's social engagement.

Hugh ushers us ahead of him into a large, high-ceilinged room full of chattering, laughing people, and Celia detaches herself from a group near the door, coming over to hug us warmly. 'Liz, darling, and Gina too, how wonderful. Grab a drink,' she says, pouring us each a glass of wine from a bottle on the table behind her, 'and come and mingle. Liz, you know everyone, I think. Gina, come with me – I simply must introduce you to Nigel.' She takes me by the hand and leads me through the throng of guests to a trio standing beside one of the windows. 'Gina Peplow, meet Sally and Oliver McKay and Nigel Yates.'

With bright smiles of something that looks suspiciously like relief, Sally and Oliver turn towards me. They've clearly been pinned down for some time by Nigel, whose pink shiny shirt matches his equally pink shiny face, topped off with what seems to be the beginnings of a comb-over. My heart sinks as Sally and Oliver, seizing the opportunity to make a break for it, mutter something about getting another drink and edge away towards the table, brutally leaving me stuck in their place. I look round for Celia, but she's already sailed off to oil the social wheels of her party elsewhere. Then I catch a glimpse of Liz across the room. She's grinning at me wickedly and raises her glass with a flourish that confirms what I've already suspected: this is a set-up.

Sighing inwardly, I turn politely to Nigel, who's enthusiastically explaining that he's new in town and asking if I live nearby. He's recently bought a wreck of a house here and is in the throes of major renovations, which he describes with gusto – and many complaints about the shortcomings of French workmen and the difficulties in finding decent plumbing fixtures – for the next half hour.

As he embarks on a detailed description of the installation of his new septic tank (with far too much information about solids, liquids and something called a leach field), I allow my gaze to wander. Liz is deep in conversation with Hugh, who leans in close to listen to something she's saying, then throws his head back to roar with laughter. I wonder idly whether perhaps he was the mystery man that she'd loved – they share the same wicked sense of humour and he's clearly always been very fond of her. Watching them together, though, I realise they are 'just good friends', in the non-euphemistic sense of the phrase. It was far more likely that Liz's unattainable lover was a rock star (Mick or Ron?) or perhaps even royalty . . .

Suddenly, I realise that Nigel's fascinating description of selected plumbing highlights has paused and he's looking at me as if expecting an answer to something he's just asked. Blushing, I say, 'I'm sorry, I didn't quite catch what you said there – terribly difficult to hear with all this din.' I gesture with my glass in a vague sweep that takes in the assembled throng.

'I just wondered whether you'd like to pop round and see the house sometime? I could show you what I've done so far.'

Tempting though the thought of a guided tour of Nigel's septic tank may be, I'm relieved to have the cast-iron excuse of my departure for home in thirty-six hours' time. Nigel looks momentarily crestfallen, but then brightens, saying, 'Never mind, we'll organise something next time you're over. There'll be even more to show you by then, I expect.'

Thankfully, Liz materialises at his shoulder, introducing herself and then saying with a smile, 'I'm sorry to have to tear Gina away, but there's someone I must introduce her to. So nice to have met you.' And she firmly takes my arm, leaving Nigel turning to a group to one side of us who look as if they need enlightening on the ins and outs (as it were) of modern sanitation systems in old French houses.

'You looked as if you needed saving,' Liz says, once we're safely out of earshot. 'What on earth was Celia thinking? She said she had a nice eligible man lined up for you.'

'Yes, I rather guessed the two of you had hatched that particular plot,' I reply, laughing, 'but next time, please don't go to any trouble on my behalf.'

'Oh, dear, this isn't exactly the richest of hunting grounds, I'm afraid. Now, do you want another glass of wine or shall we bow out graciously and get home for supper?'

'Well, unless you and Celia have another hot date lined up for me, I think a cheese omelette and a good book sound like bliss . . .'

The next day is my last full day in France before I drive north to catch the overnight ferry home. Saturday is market day in Sainte-Foy-la-Grande and we spend a happy couple of hours browsing among the stalls of cheeses, oysters, spices and pyramids of fresh, colourful fruit and vegetables. We manage to find a free table at the café in the corner of the square and sink into two chairs, Liz's large wicker basket at our feet, overflowing with fresh produce and neat greaseproof-paper-wrapped parcels. As I blow on the frothy surface of my *grand crème*, a familiar pink face appears through the crowd, waving enthusiastically.

'Aha, I've tracked you down,' crows Nigel. 'I thought you two lovely ladies might be here this morning.' He looks around for a chair to pull up to our table but, luckily for us, there are none free on the crowded pavement in front of the café. Unabashed, with a flourish he pulls a small card out of his shirt pocket. 'Thought I'd give you my contact details. Let me know next time you're coming over and we'll get something in the diary. I can show you over the house, give you some lunch or whatever.' Politely, and concentrating hard on avoiding catching Liz's eye, I take the card.

'Thanks,' I say lamely. 'That's a really kind thought.'

'Well, must be going,' says Nigel. 'My bathroom tiles aren't going to grout themselves.' I agree that this does indeed sound unlikely, and we shake hands. '*Au revoir* and *à bientôt* then, as we say here,' he beams, and disappears through the crowd.

'Well,' says Liz, 'you certainly seem to have made an impression there!'

'Hmm, yes. The fact that there isn't another available Anglo-Saxon female under the age of sixty for about five hundred miles has nothing to do with it, of course.'

'Nonsense. Don't put yourself down. Although come to think of it, it was probably that vintage top of mine that did it,' grins Liz. 'It did look good on you. Now, come on, let's go home and get this food put away.'

After lunch that day I drag a pair of battered sun loungers out of the woodshed and set them up on the terrace, dusting off their winter wrapping of sticky strands of spiders' web. We sit side by side, lifting our faces to the sun, Liz with the local newspaper,

Sud-Ouest, and me with my book. After a while I rest the book on my stomach, closing my eyes for just a minute . . .

I wake with a start sometime later, the hoarse screech of a magpie rousing me from my sleep. I swivel the watch on my wrist to squint at the time, noticing that the strap has made a faint white stripe against the pale gold of my skin after a day or two of French sun. It's nearly four o'clock and the sun lounger next to me is deserted. I ease myself up stiffly, straightening my creased T-shirt, my mouth sticky with the staleness of the deep sleep of afternoon. Going into the house, I find Liz back in her study, sifting through papers on her lap.

'Cup of tea?' I ask.

'Lovely,' she replies vaguely, deep in some old letters. She perches her glasses on top of her head and looks up with a smile. 'You were out for the count.'

'I know. Fresh air and good food are so exhausting. I seem to be making up for all the sleep I've lost of late. It's bliss!'

I put the tea things on a tin tray and carry them through to the study, where Liz reaches to clear a space on a small table, piling folders on to the floor.

'You're inspiring me to have a good spring clean when I get home,' I say. 'I still haven't quite got round to carrying out my New Year's resolution of decluttering both my wardrobe and the flat. Minimalist chic will be my new watchword.' I hand Liz a pretty bone china cup and saucer. 'Earl Grey, no milk – that right?'

'Perfect,' she smiles. 'Minimalist chic, eh? Not sure that's really your style. Chic yes, minimalist no. And anyway, that's two watchwords.'

I turn to pour my own cup of tea, settling myself in a sagging armchair, distracted by a pile of *Vogue* magazines from the late sixties. Reaching for one, I say, 'Maybe I can find some inspiration here. That top you gave me could be the start of a whole new image.

What do you think?' I'm leafing through the magazine, but there's no reply from Liz.

Glancing up, I notice that my aunt is sitting with her gaze fixed on the air in front of her. 'Liz?' I say. And then again more sharply, 'Liz!'

I jump to my feet as, still with a fixed gaze, she tilts slightly to one side and the cup and saucer fall clattering to the floor at her feet, splattering papers and photographs with hot tea.

I grab her arm and kneel down in front of her, shaking her shoulder and looking up into the fixed, faraway mask of her face. Slowly her eyes focus on mine and expression returns, a flicker of fear mirroring the terror that must be written on my face, before she gives a little start and tries to draw herself up to sit straight again in her chair.

'Oh, dear,' she says faintly. 'Don't know what came over me there. Such a silly thing to do. Look what a mess I've made.'

'Never mind that, I'll clean it up. But are you okay? What happened? Did you feel faint?'

'I just blacked out for a second, I think. Must have got a bit too much sun earlier.'

She tries to stand and sways dizzily. I help her to her feet, an arm round her shoulders, which feel especially fragile and bony through the thin cotton of her blouse.

'Come on, let's get you upstairs. You'd better have a bit of a lie-down.'

In her room I settle her on her bed, slipping off her shoes and easing her feet, lumpy with bunions, on to the coverlet. I sit on the bed beside her, holding her hand.

'Look at you,' she smiles, a little shakily. 'I've frightened the living daylights out of you. Don't worry, it's just one of my turns. Part of the joys of old age.'

I stay with her, stroking the thin, age-spotted skin on the back of her hand as she drifts asleep.

Looking round her room, I take in the framed photos that have hung on these walls for as long as I can remember. They're all of birds – the bright eye, curved beak and exotic crest of a hoopoe; a grey heron tiptoeing on stick-like legs through a reed bed in the river; a black-and-white print of a long 'V' of grey cranes flying north in the spring, looking and sounding like creaky barn doors with their vast wingspans and rusty, honking cries.

Listening to her faint but regular breathing, my eye falls on a picture in a heavy silver frame on her bedside cabinet. I can't remember having seen this one before. It's another black-and-white photo and I recognise the outline of a cedar tree that stands beside the drive. On it, at the ends of six of its branches, are perched three pairs of magpies, their black-and-white plumage sitting within the symmetry of the tree, like neatly placed decorations on a Christmas tree. The rhyme popped into my head again. 'Six for gold,' I think to myself with a smile. 'In a frame of silver.' Trust Liz to see the beauty in the moment and be able to catch it on camera. It must appeal to her quirky sense of humour to have it sitting here beside her bed.

Lafite comes through the door on silent paws and jumps smoothly on to a chair on the other side of the bed. He settles down to watch us, eyes narrowed, and I feel reassured by his presence.

Checking again that Liz's breathing is quiet and regular, I leave her under the watchful gaze of the black cat and creep out of the room to go and clear up the spilt tea in the study.

Later, I tap on her bedroom door to ask if she'd like me to bring her supper up on a tray. She's awake, lying on her side and gazing at the photo of the magpies beside her. She turns and smiles. 'Some soup would be lovely, thanks. I'm feeling fine now. I think I'll come down. Give me a hand getting up?'

As we sit over our supper at the kitchen table, I say, 'I'm worried about leaving you tomorrow. If you've had these blackouts before then I really think you should go and see a doctor. Will you promise me you'll phone first thing on Monday morning? You should see your GP and you might need to be referred to a specialist.'

'I'll be fine,' says Liz. 'I'll call Mireille if I start feeling funny again. She's a minute up the lane if I need her. In any case, she looks in every day to say hello when she knows I don't have anyone here. So don't worry, she's keeping an eye on me. And I'm honestly feeling okay now.'

'Yes, but promise me you'll go and see the doctor,' I insist.

'You young things are very bossy nowadays,' she laughs, shaking her head, and I'm relieved to hear a little of the usual spark back in her voice.

'And you slightly less-young things are very stubborn,' I retort. 'Promise me.'

'Okay, okay.' She holds up her hands in mock surrender. 'I promise.'

◆ ◆ ◆

It reassures me to find her looking a good deal more like herself the next day. As I drive away, the last thing I see in my rear-view mirror is the slight figure of my beloved aunt, standing beneath the cedar tree and waving me goodbye.

Chapter 3

I've hardly been back a fortnight, after the buying trip to France, when my mother calls me with the news. I realise that, in some dark recess of my mind, I've known this was coming, but have been studiously ignoring it. Like a child who puts their hands over their eyes believing that if they can't see the monster, the monster can't see them.

I'm sitting at my kitchen table as my mother tells me the news of my aunt's death, a shopping list I've been writing in front of me. Bread, it says. Eggs, milk, washing-up liquid. Frozen in shock and grief, the words burn themselves into my dry eyes, mundane and meaningless. Mum's voice over the phone is calm and composed, and for a moment I think I've fallen through a hole in time and am listening to her telling me of my father's death a year before. She'd been so cool and collected then too, and it upset me how remote she seemed from him, in death as in life; their marriage had always appeared to be more one of convenience than passion.

But I force myself to listen to the words she is saying now and this time they're different.

'A neighbour found her yesterday afternoon. A stroke, they think, very sudden. Celia Everett called to tell me. She and Hugh are being wonderful getting everything organised at that end, which is a huge help as their French is so good and they're on the spot.

The funeral should be towards the end of the week. Apparently Liz left instructions.'

My throat and chest constrict with the crushing pain of grief and loss. It hurts to speak.

'She knew it was coming,' I say dully. A sudden vision flashes into my mind of Liz in her study during my last visit, sorting through piles of papers. And then I remember the heaps of clothes in her bedroom, and the roll of black bin bags. A spring clean, she'd said. And I think of the vintage top she insisted on giving me, now hanging in my wardrobe, and a sob escapes me like an air bubble rising up from the deep ocean floor.

'Oh, Gina, darling,' says my mother. 'I know how much she meant to you. Stay where you are, I'm coming over.'

I place the phone carefully on the table in front of me, its outline swimming as my tears fall, blurring the ink on the shopping list beside it. I'm still sitting there, numb and shivering, when Mum rings the doorbell half an hour later. The world has become a colder place without my aunt in it.

◆ ◆ ◆

The cremation has been arranged for the Friday afternoon and we're met at Bergerac airport the evening before by Hugh Everett. 'Of course you'll stay with us,' Celia had insisted during one of the many phone calls she and my mother had exchanged over the course of the week. I would have far preferred to stay in Liz's house, but that idea was swept briskly aside by the formidable organisational task force (Sussex and Gironde branches) that had taken charge of matters.

As we sit in beautifully upholstered (Sanderson chintz) armchairs in the Everetts' beautifully decorated (Farrow & Ball) sitting room, sipping gin and tonics out of beautifully sparkling

27

(Edinburgh crystal) glasses, Celia clasps a hand to her own beautifully upholstered (cashmere and pearls) bosom and sighs deeply. 'Such a shock for us all, a terrible loss. And especially hard for you, Gina; we know how close you were to Liz and how fond she was of you.' She pauses and looks across at Hugh, who has just sat down on the sofa beside Mum and is in the process of taking a long and thankful draught of his drink. 'Darling,' she prompts, 'I think you have something to tell Gina?'

'Yes, indeed.' Hugh turns to me. 'Liz had everything extremely well organised. A while ago she asked me to be an executor of her will, and I'm pleased to tell you, Gina, that she has left her entire estate to you. Not that it amounts to much – it's really just the house and its contents. She had a little money invested to give her an annuity, and her state pension of course. And there's the occasional royalty from her books and photos, but that's just a trickle these days. The house is worth a bob or two, though, if you want to sell. Needs a bit doing to it, of course, but around here you can usually find an expat looking for a project to take on.'

It's all moving too fast for me to take in. My immediate reaction is, 'No way am I selling Liz's house,' but then I pull myself up short. 'But, Mum, shouldn't some of this come to you?'

'Oh, darling, that's so sweet of you, but no. I really don't need more than I have. Your father left me very comfortably provided for, as you know. Of course Liz wanted you to have this, and quite right too. Just think what it would mean if you sold the house. You could use the money to pay off the mortgage on your flat, or to move up the property ladder and invest in something a little more desirable. It's a lovely opportunity.'

My aunt's dead body is lying in a funeral home a few miles away and her own sister is sitting here, in the lamplit warmth of Celia's elegant drawing room, coolly talking about selling her house and it being a 'lovely opportunity'. I love my mother dearly, but honestly, at times she can be so cold. I feel my face flushing and my eyes filling with angry tears at her heartlessness as she prattles on about selling the house.

Celia may be sharp and sometimes overbearing, but she's also kindly and perspicacious and she sees how wretched I'm feeling. 'Well now' – she pats my arm – 'there's more than enough time for you to think things over. You don't have to make any decisions in a hurry and anyway it'll take a while for the *notaire* to sort out all the paperwork. Let it sink in. We'll keep popping in to check the house now and then, and of course Liz's neighbour, Madame Thibault, keeps an eye on the place. She's taken in the cat, Lafite, you know. Apparently he was sitting beside Liz's body when Mireille Thibault found her, as if he was watching over her until help arrived. It was really very touching.'

I remember meeting Mireille the last time I stayed with Liz, and feel a little better at the thought of her taking care of things.

In a daze of emotional exhaustion, I choke down a little supper and then take myself off to bed. Despite all the little comforting touches Celia's provided – a vase of fresh flowers, a bottle of mineral water, some relaxing bath oil – I feel empty and decidedly un-comforted. Lying under the quilted coverlet in the Everetts' second spare room (my mother is down the hall in the main guest suite), I spend a sleepless night, wishing I was in Liz's spare room – my spare room now – so that I could have felt closer to her on this last night her body is on the Earth.

◆ ◆ ◆

The crematorium is as drab and depressing as these places are the world over. Liz had left very specific instructions, and Hugh and Celia have arranged everything accordingly. The coffin is the plainest pine, but I place an armful of scented white lilies on it, my farewell gift to my aunt.

When we enter the room where the service is to be conducted, my eyes swim as I make out a crowded blur of faces. Despite Liz's directive that her funeral was to be small, with no fuss, she couldn't deter the many friends, both French and English, who have turned up to see her off. I catch sight of Mireille Thibault, waiting patiently to one side as a few of the assembled throng come up to offer their sympathies. She puts her arms round me in a warm embrace, saying nothing, and for the first time since hearing the news of Liz's death I feel comforted. Overwhelmed, I stay in the circle of her arms for a minute until, patting my back gently, she pulls back and her bright, wise old eyes look into mine. 'You'll be coming to the house this weekend?' she asks. 'Come and knock on my door. Lafite will be pleased to see you.'

'Are you coming back to the Everetts' after the service? They're having a reception and you'll be most welcome.'

'Thank you, but no. I'm just going to say my *adieus* to Liz here and then go home. But I'll see you tomorrow. *Bon courage*, my dear.'

And courage is exactly what I need half an hour later, as the coffin slides silently through the curtain and my beloved aunt is gone.

◆　◆　◆

The day after the funeral, Celia and my mother drop me off at the end of the lane and drive away down the hill, to the bustle of the Saturday morning market in Sainte-Foy and, no doubt, a lingering gossip over a coffee in the square.

It's a beautiful spring day and I walk up the lane between the neat vines, which are just beginning to weave themselves into a lush tapestry along their supporting wires. Pink and purple orchids nestle in the long grass beside the verge and the musical chatter of birdsong floats on the breeze.

I pass the end of Liz's driveway and continue on as far as Mireille's cottage at the edge of the plum orchard. On the gravel in front of the door, among pots of cheerful red geraniums, a little girl sits stroking Lafite, who's stretched himself out luxuriously to bask in the warmth of the sun. As I walk up the path, the old cat jumps to his feet and comes to greet me, purring and winding himself around my shins. The little girl watches me for a moment, and I have a fleeting impression of serious brown eyes, set in a pale heart-shaped face framed by straight brown hair. She turns and darts into the house, reappearing a few seconds later with Mireille.

'Gina, my dear, how are you?' Mireille kisses me on each cheek before enveloping me in a warm hug. She looks at my face searchingly. 'Yesterday was a sad day, but today is a little more peaceful I think?' She ushers the little girl forward. 'May I present my granddaughter, Nathalie.' The child turns her face upwards for the customary two kisses.

'Lafite was very much enjoying being stroked by you,' I smile.

'Yes,' she says. 'He is missing Liz' – she pronounces it *Lees* – 'but I am helping Mamie Mireille look after him and cheer him up.'

'Well, thank you. He couldn't be among better friends.'

'Shall we come to the house with you?' asks Mireille.

I had planned to go on my own, but suddenly the thought of stepping over the threshold alone into that emptiness overwhelms me. 'Yes, please, I'd like that.'

And the company is just what I need, I realise, as Nathalie and Lafite dance ahead of us, scattering any ghosts, and Mireille's calm presence at my side dispels the post-funeral loneliness I had been feeling.

To my relief, the house is pervaded by an air of peace and I feel surprisingly reassured to be standing in the familiar kitchen once again, the steady tick of the clock on the mantel above the fireplace marking time as if nothing has changed.

'She was lying here on the floor when I found her,' says Mireille softly. 'I'd come over for my customary cup of afternoon tea. It was Liz who introduced me to this most civilised of English customs. The kettle was still warm, so she couldn't have been there long.

'I think she sensed it was coming. She'd been getting things organised for the past few months. I helped her take some bags to the dump, and others, of clothes and whatever else might be of use, to the church. It was important to her to leave everything in order.'

Tears spring to my eyes. 'When I was here, she wasn't well. I told her to go to the doctor. I should have stayed, taken her to the hospital maybe . . .'

Mireille puts a steadying hand on my arm. 'Which she would have refused to do.' She smiles at me and hands me a tissue from her pocket. 'You know how strong-minded your aunt always was – stubborn as a mule. She'd made up her mind and wanted to do this on her own terms. She got what she had hoped for, which was a wonderful quality of life right up to the end, and to die in her own home. Not in a hospital, full of tubes, nor to moulder in a nursing home among strangers. She was ready to go, you know.'

We wander through the rooms, where everything is neatly ordered. The heaps of papers that used to cover every surface have disappeared from the study, leaving just a set of well-ordered files on the bookshelves that line one wall. I take a look in one. It's full of old negatives in plastic sleeves. One day I'll go through them. Perhaps I should offer them to an archive somewhere that might be interested in keeping them.

Only a few items of clothing hang in the wardrobe in Liz's bedroom.

'She just kept what she might need from day to day,' explains Mireille. 'Would you like me to clear out these last few things and take them to the church? It's a sad job, getting rid of something as personal as clothes, and so it might be easier for me to do. As long as you and your mother don't want any of it, of course.'

I think of Mum's elegantly conservative clothes in neutral colours, a far cry from Liz's more flamboyant taste. 'I'd be grateful, if you wouldn't mind doing it,' I reply. 'I already have a few things that she gave me to remember her by.'

We make our way back down to the kitchen. Nathalie and Lafite, bored at the thought of wasting time inside, are in the court-yard. The cat watches, with eagle eyes, a lizard that has plastered itself to the wall. The little girl sits on the step making daisy chains.

Then, with a crunch of gravel, Celia's car pulls up and the peace of the moment is shattered.

We discuss practicalities for a while – Celia and Mireille between them will keep an eye on things until the lawyer had final-ised the will and I've decided what to do with the house.

'Take your time, my dear,' says Mireille as she takes her leave. 'It meant a lot to Liz to leave you the house, but she didn't want it to be a burden. You must do whatever you feel is right for you.'

And I watch as the old lady makes her way down the drive, accompanied by the black cat, and the little girl wearing a crown of daisies.

Chapter 4

Coming back to the office after Liz's funeral, my mind is still in France. The sunshine and birdsong of the French countryside seem more real than the grey English sky and the Monday morning grumble of high-street traffic.

I settle down at my desk, trying to focus on work, opening my notebook to today's to-do list, which is dauntingly long. The office door bangs open and Annie crashes into the room, breathless and laughing at some exchange she'd just had with the staff in the shop downstairs. She's the buyer for New World wines and is as voluptuous, brash, loud and warm-hearted as many of the products in her portfolio.

'Hooray, Gina, you're back! Did it all go okay?' She holds me at arm's length for a moment, scanning my face to see how I'm really doing, then hugs me warmly. 'Got time for a drink after work tonight? Good. I need to tell you all about the most gorgeous man I've just met.'

'I like the hair,' I say. Annie changes her hair colour about as often as she changes her men. Which is very often. When I'd left the previous week, she'd been a redhead. She's now a dramatically dark brunette. But with Annie Mackenzie, one always senses that blondeness is never very far away.

I settle down to work and, on automatic pilot, I open my emails and realise I'm reading one from Ed. 'So sorry to hear of your aunt's death – saw her obit. Presume you must be in France. Thinking of you. Love E.'

It's the 'Love E' that really gets my attention.

It's been over a month since we split up.

As I'm mulling this over, my phone beeps with an incoming text message, and I fish it out of my bag. From: Ed. 'Call me when u get this. X'.

Heavens, what's going on? Love Ed? A kiss? After weeks of radio silence. I'm confused. I click the message shut, then sit staring at the computer screen for a few seconds before reopening the email to scan it again. Whichever way you look at it, it's a definite invitation to reopen lines of contact. Hah, maybe he's realised what he's missing now his 'bit on the side' has moved to a more central – and no doubt less exciting – position. He moved out of my flat and into Camilla's in Pimlico in one smooth step, smoothness always having been one of Ed's most obvious character traits.

But perhaps now he'd broken it off with her, I think, and I imagine a highly satisfactory scene where we meet up and he'll be contrite, begging me to take him back. Naturally, being strong-minded and highly principled, I'll turn him down. But then after a suitable period of begging and a campaign involving several large bouquets of flowers, boxes of chocolates, etc., he'll convince me that he's a changed man and we'll be together again, happily ever after.

I snap myself out of my reverie with a shake of my head. 'Yeah, and watch out for flying pigs, too,' I mutter under my breath.

I'm still in a state of distraction, though, when Harry Wainright leans out of his office and says, 'Gina, can I ask you to come through, please?'

And so it hardly sinks in at first when he tells me that the company has been bought by one of the big chains.

Then he drops the bombshell. 'I'm sorry, Gina, and I know the timing couldn't be worse with all you've been going through, but I'm going to have to let you go.'

◆　◆　◆

At the end of the awful day when I hear I've lost my job, I relent and call Ed. I feel as though I've lost everything that matters – Dad, Liz, my job. Drowning in grief, shock and despondency, those messages he's sent out of the blue seem as though he's holding out an emotional life jacket to me just when I need it most. My self-esteem is at an all-time low and I've never felt so alone. Perhaps it wouldn't hurt to talk, at least, I tell myself. After all, everyone deserves a second chance, don't they? He's sympathetic when I tell him the news about losing my job and seems genuinely concerned. 'You need cheering up,' he says. 'Can I buy you dinner sometime?'

We meet a few days later in the local Italian restaurant, familiar territory since we used to go there on Friday nights to celebrate the end of the working week, relaxing over plates of spaghetti puttanesca and a bottle of house plonk. Ed is already there when I arrive – notable in itself, as he is usually late as a matter of course – and stands up solicitously to embrace me as I reach the table. He orders a bottle of wine, a Barolo from the top end of the wine list, I notice, rather than our usual Valpolicella, and I'm pleased and cautiously flattered that he's making such an effort. Where is this going, I wonder, trying to ignore the glow of hope that has rekindled itself in my heart. Have he and Camilla split up? I'd forgotten how very good-looking he is, and how utterly charming he can be when not otherwise distracted. I ask Ed, with a smile of irony at the normality of the question after the turmoil I've been through in the last seven days, how his week has been.

Ed is Director of Sponsorship for an events company. When you come down to it, this means he sells advertising. The job mainly involves wining and dining contacts made through the Old Boy networks of the public schools of southern England and persuading them, in the most gentlemanly manner, to part with large dollops of money to have their companies' names displayed at polo matches, rugby fixtures and regattas. Apparently, at the moment things aren't going too well, and it has been proving, Ed admits over his bresaola and rocket salad, to be a bit of a bore of late.

'But that's enough about me. More importantly, how are you?' he asks, reaching a sympathetic hand across the table to hold mine.

The glow of hope in me flickers into a small flame.

'I was so sorry to hear about your job. Still, in the big scheme of things, it's funny how it's worked out really, isn't it? You've obviously reached an important crossroads in your life. What are you planning on doing next, now you have carte blanche?'

I'm surprised that he sees my current situation in quite such exciting and positive terms, but Ed's always been an optimist. Perhaps he's right – I should see this as an opportunity for a fresh start rather than having the distinct feeling that I'm being swept rapidly up a certain well-known creek without a paddle.

He gazes across at me over the tea light and the bottles of oil and vinegar as I describe the calls I've been making and the copies of my CV I've sent out, completely fruitlessly. 'So it looks like I'm going to be unemployed for the foreseeable future.' I try to make light of my situation, which actually sounds even more dire to me when I have to explain it like this.

The waiter appears with our plates of pasta and then suggestively brandishes an oversized pepper grinder in my direction.

'Pepper for the *bella signorina*?' Ed waves him away and pours me some more of the dark red wine.

'Well, I'd like to propose a toast,' he says, with a flourish of his own glass. 'Here's to ladies of leisure. I was sorry to hear about your Aunt Liz, of course, but talk about good timing. Presumably she's left everything to you? Bit of a silver lining as it turns out, eh?'

For a few seconds I continue to smile, as I try to work out what he could possibly mean. And then, as realisation dawns, a wave of icy-cold water washes over the blaze of hope that, I have to admit, has by now been burning brightly within me, extinguishing it completely.

'I'm sorry?' I say frostily. 'I'm not sure I quite follow.'

Ed continues breezily, 'Well, she must have been pretty minted, and you were certainly her nearest and dearest relation, just like a daughter in fact, so surely she's come up trumps just when you need it most. I always did like the old girl – a great character.'

His mobile phone, on the pink tablecloth beside a half-eaten breadstick, suddenly vibrates. He glances down at it and then smoothly – too smoothly – returns his gaze to my face. 'Gina?' he asks, as I glare at him in cold fury.

I reach over and pick up his phone. On the screen is a little envelope and next to it the name *Camilla*.

'Ah, yes,' I say, 'how is the lovely Camilla these days? Still your landlady? Or did you finally strap on a pair and decide to stand on your own two feet for a change? No?' I continue, as his gaze flickers uncertainly to the plate of food in front of him. 'So you're still living with her, but thought it would be worth checking me out again in case I'd suddenly become a better financial proposition? I should have known. The trouble with you, Edmund Cavendish, is that you are, and always will be, a complete arsehole. Thanks for supper, but sorry, I've just remembered I'd rather be at home scrubbing the mould off the shower curtain than waste one more second of my life in your company.'

Shaking with rage, I push back my chair and stalk out of the restaurant, Italian waiters with their oversized pepper grinders scattering before me as I go. Not such a *bella signorina* after all, evidently.

And my fury propels me to my front door and up the stairs to my flat before I collapse on the sofa and lie there, unable to move, as I contemplate what an idiot I've been to think I might give Ed a second chance. I should have known – he's the last person to offer any support in the twisted pile of wreckage that my life has become.

◆　◆　◆

After that ghastly evening with Ed, when I finally have proof – if more were needed – of what a complete loser he is, I've plummeted into a deep depression. With no work to go to, I spend my time lying on the sofa eating my body weight in chocolate HobNobs and watching old episodes of *Bargain Hunt* on TV. The odd glimmer of hope comes when an envelope lands on the doormat in response to one of the job applications I've submitted, only to be dashed as the words of yet another polite rejection swim before my eyes and I reach for one more biscuit to numb the pain.

I'm in grave danger of becoming an expert on art deco ceramics and developing a backside the size of the Bay of Biscay.

The days are bad enough, but I particularly dread the nights, contemplating each one with trepidation as it stretches before me, a dark desert to be crossed alone, knowing that in the shadows my anxious thoughts lurk, waiting to ambush me and harry me, nipping at my heels like a pack of wild dogs. Some evenings I drift asleep in front of the television before dragging myself groggily into bed an hour or so later, only to lie there wider awake than ever the minute my head hits the pillow. Sometimes, relieved that another restless night is over, I fall into a deep sleep just as dawn breaks, floundering in a quicksand of troubled dreams that relinquish their grip on my mind only reluctantly when I wake, leaving me feeling queasy and emotionally drained.

One of these dreams stays with me with particular clarity. In it, I'm trying to get to France – I have to get to France to see Liz urgently – but am held up at every turn. First, I have work to finish (ha!), then I jump into a taxi to get to the airport, only to find Ed sitting in it. He insists we go back to his place to pick up his suitcase. I realise we've missed the plane, so I go to catch a bus to the station, but there's one just pulling away and I run to catch it but my legs are like lead weights and my lungs constrict so that I can hardly move. I push on, though, and get to the station. The Eurostar is – miraculously – still there and I go to buy a ticket. But there's a long queue and it's not moving. I crane my head to see who's holding it up and Ed turns to smile at me from the front of the line. Weak-kneed with relief, I go up to him, but he turns away. Then I see he has bought two tickets and I know the second one is not for me. In desperation, I get on the train anyway just as it pulls away from the platform. But instead of whizzing soundlessly through the countryside, it seems to have developed the same problem as my legs, and drags itself along laboriously. I get out and miraculously find myself at Sainte-Foy – hooray, nearly there, hang on Liz, I'm coming. I force my leaden limbs to carry me up the hill and finally I turn into the drive under the oaks. But the courtyard is empty and the trees are skeletons and I know I'm too late. All I can hear is my desperate, gasping breath and then a magpie flutters down from one of the trees and stalks towards me with menacing intent. It gives a rasping cry and I wake with a start.

The last time I dream that dream, I hit rock bottom.

I wake, gasping for breath, to find that there really is a magpie calling in the trees in one of the neighbouring gardens.

I lie there for a while, trying to calm my breathing and gather my thoughts. I need to get a grip. How do you know when you're losing it? Is this what a nervous breakdown feels like?

I get up and go through to the kitchen. Opening the fridge door, I gaze at an unappetising heel of stale bread and a single pot of yoghurt, which, on closer inspection, turns out to be about a week past its sell-by date. I reach for the biscuit tin, but there's nothing in it apart from the forlorn wrapper from a packet of HobNobs.

The phone is lying on the counter beside me and, almost without thinking, I pick it up and dial. 'Hi, Mum,' I say, 'how are you?'

'Oh, hello darling, just getting ready to go out, actually. What are you doing today?'

'Nothing much. Just wondering if I could pop over sometime?'

'Well, I'm going shopping this morning and then I've got bridge this afternoon,' she replies breezily.

'Okay, well, another day then.' I try hard to keep the tremor in my voice from spilling over into something unstoppable.

There's a pause.

'Are you all right, darling?'

I swallow hard and suddenly find that I can't get the words out because if I open my mouth I'll start to cry and I don't think I'll ever be able to stop.

'Actually, the shopping can wait,' says my mother briskly into the silence that hums over the airwaves between us. 'Come straight over. Or shall I come to you instead?'

I take a deep breath. 'I'll come to you. Be nice to have a change of scene,' I say into the phone with a watery smile.

Half an hour later, Mum is putting two mugs of coffee on a tray beside a Royal Doulton plate bearing some leftover home baking from her latest bridge afternoon. The familiarity and home-liness are comforting.

'It's such a lovely day, let's take this into the garden,' she says.

Instead of sitting on the patio next to the house, she leads the way across the lawn to Dad's bench. We sit and she offers me the plate of cakes. I shake my head and she says kindly, 'Come on, Gina, you look as if you haven't eaten properly in days. Or slept either, come to that. Take one and tell me what's on your mind.' Balancing her mug of coffee on the arm of the bench, she reaches over and takes my hand.

And we sit there for a while as the tears pour silently down my face and she waits patiently and calmly until the torrent turns to a trickle.

Then, releasing my hand, she pulls a neatly folded handkerchief from her sleeve and passes it to me. 'My poor darling girl,' she says, which sets me off again, but I'm almost cried out now, so after a minute or two I blow my nose and find that the oppressive weight of my grief, which had been crushing my heart into a lump as dense and heavy as lead, has been washed away in the flood and now I'm left empty and exhausted, but calmer.

'I think I'm going to have to sell Liz's house,' I blurt out, gazing sightlessly at the blue of the southerly skies before us. 'If I sell it, I can pay off the mortgage on the flat, so at least I won't lose that as well. Then hopefully my redundancy money will tide me over, if I'm careful, until I can find another job.'

My mother looks at me appraisingly. 'I see. Is that really what you want to do? It doesn't sound much fun to me.'

Fun? I bite my tongue in order not to snap her head off. She's never had to worry about money so she has no idea what it's like for those of us out in the real world.

Overwhelmed with self-pity, I sniff and then blow my nose again on the crumpled handkerchief, which I'm still clutching in my fist. 'Well, I don't exactly have any choices at the moment,' I say bitterly.

'Nonsense, darling. Choices are exactly what you have. I think this is a wonderful opportunity for you.' I start to interrupt, but she holds up a hand. 'Now hear me out. I know you've been through a horrible time, and I'm not surprised you're knocked sideways. You must feel as if you've lost absolutely everything.'

A sob escapes me and she takes my hand again.

'But, in reality, you've gained enormous freedom and that's not something that happens to everyone in life. This is a chance for you to go where you want and do something completely different.'

A pair of gulls wheel overhead, blown inland by a freshening wind from the south, and I watch the trajectory of their flight as they soar higher, then turn back towards the sea beyond the rolling hills. Freedom's just another word for nothing left to lose, as the words of the song go.

Maybe Mum's right. I am free now, as free as a bird. And while it's terrifying, perhaps it could also be exhilarating to spread my wings and fly, a chance to try something new. I think of my father, how he used to come and sit on this very bench, feeling the breeze on his face as he watched the swallows in the evening light. Shortly before he died, he asked me whether I was happy in my job, saying, 'There's a whole wide world out there for you to explore, Gina. You could study for a Master of Wine qualification and once you have it you could go anywhere you like.'

I know how tough the MW course is. At the time I'd dismissed the idea, safe in my job at Wainright's and, to be honest, a bit scared of the idea of trying and failing. Of letting Dad down as well as myself. But now, suddenly, it seems like the best idea I've had in a long while. The southerly breeze feels like a messenger sent from the other side of the Channel, and a plan begins to formulate itself in my head.

As if she's read my mind, Mum takes my hand again and says, 'Go and spend some time in France. You have somewhere to stay that you love. Your redundancy money will tide you over for a while. Dad always said you should get your Master of Wine qualification and you can easily do it from there and come back to sit the exams when you're ready. Indeed, what better place could there be to immerse yourself in wine? Within reason, of course,' she finishes with a smile.

We sit in silence for a few seconds while I take all this in. Then I voice my self-doubts. 'But Mum, what if I try and fail?'

She turns to face me. 'Oh my darling, but what if you try and fly?'

Then she looks off into the distance, her expression unreadable. 'Dad would have given you the same advice, you know. He'd have been delighted if you got your MW. Now,' she says, reverting to her usual businesslike manner as she gathers up the mugs and tray, 'I'm going to leave you to sit in the sun and think things over while I get our lunch ready.'

A while later, as I take my leave, I hug my mother warmly. 'Thanks, Mum,' I say, and she smiles and strokes the side of my face with a gesture that's utterly tender.

'You're a gorgeous girl, Gina, and a wonderful daughter. I'm so proud of you, you know. You have opportunities that I never did – I just want you to see that and make the most of them. Now, get back out there and start living.' Then she bends her head to rummage in her bag for her car keys.

So we go our separate ways – my mother to go off to her afternoon of bridge, sandwiches and small talk, and I to get a life.

Chapter 5

A fresh start. Like Mum said, that's something we don't often get in life, a completely clean slate. Although to be honest, the blankness of that clean slate is just a little terrifying when you've been used to having your days filled by a full-time job, with a steady salary and a busy social life on which to spend it.

As I drive south towards my new home, the car crammed with my worldly belongings and a dozen packets of chocolate HobNobs (essential survival rations), I can hear Liz's voice, encouraging me, telling me I'm doing the right thing. Perhaps her spirit is with me on the journey. That thought calms me a bit and gives me confidence as I leave behind my familiar life in England for the unknown here in France.

I'll need to create a new structure for myself out here, I decide. A healthy and balanced lifestyle of exercise, good diet, wine only in moderation (although admittedly that one could be tricky, given that I'm going to be living in one of the biggest and best wine regions of the world), and some serious studying for my Master of Wine qualification. I will use this opportunity as a sabbatical for some intensive self-improvement, returning to England tanned, toned and well qualified, with a newly acquired air of French sophistication, in order to relaunch myself into my stratospheric career in the London wine trade. I stifle the fear and the self-doubt and all the thoughts of why this move might be a terrible idea and try to concentrate on being a poised, worldly traveller instead.

Not much further to go now. I negotiate the series of round-abouts on the ring road that skirts Sainte-Foy and then take the road that winds up the hill, tracing the route I'd followed in my troubled dreams. It's going to be strange living in Liz's house – I still can't think of it as mine. My mind goes back to the last couple of times I've been here, to that final visit before Liz's death and then the numb, grief-filled blur of her funeral.

Lost in my thoughts, I nearly miss the turning into the lane between the vines. I swerve at the last moment, the car slewing sideways as I just manage to make the turn.

And then I have to stand on the brakes with all my force as I come face to face with a dark-blue pickup that's coming down the narrow lane towards me. My tyres screech and skid on a patch of loose gravel and, as if in slow motion, the back end of the car slides gracefully into the ditch. The engine stalls and I sit in sudden silence, shaking all over at my narrow miss. So near and yet so far – I'm only a few yards from the driveway to Liz's house and here I am, disastrously stuck in what I can only wish was a proverbial rut but sadly and incredibly annoyingly turns out to be a real one.

There's a tap on my window. The driver of the pickup has jumped down from his cab and run over. He peers in at me and I have an impression of warm eyes in a deeply tanned face. I roll down the window.

'*Excusez-moi*, Madame,' he says, concerned. 'Are you all right?'

I don't know whether to laugh or cry. I'm shaken, but unhurt. I nod, covered in embarrassment. 'Just stuck.' I open the door and try to clamber out but the angle is awkward with the backside of the car in the ditch and its nose in the air. I miss my footing and almost end up on my own backside, slipping on to my knees and covering my jeans with mud in the process. Not the most dignified of entrances.

'*Oopla!*' says the man, clutching my arm with a strong hand and helping me back on to my feet. He grins widely, obviously highly amused at my predicament and my increasingly dishevelled state, then hunkers down to get a closer look at the back wheels.

'Don't worry – I'll be able to tow you out of there. No damage done, fortunately. You were going far too fast for these small roads.'

I bristle slightly. Listen, mate, I want to say, the last thing I need right now is a lecture from a smug, know-it-all Frenchman. I've been travelling for twenty-four hours, have lost my job, my boyfriend, and most of my family, haven't slept properly in months, have had to up sticks and move so far from my comfort zone that I can't even remember what my comfort zone looks like any more, and now I and all my worldly goods have ended up in a muddy ditch. So it hasn't exactly been my day, has it?

But I don't say this, partly because my French isn't up to it and partly because I manage to remind myself just in time that he is the one with the tow rope and the four-wheel drive. And so, unless I want to leave my car stuck here and carry everything I own up the drive to my new home one cardboard box and bin-bagful at a time, I had better be polite.

I smile and manage a faint, '*Merci,* Monsieur,' as he fixes the rope under the car. I clamber awkwardly back into the driver's seat and then he carefully edges his pickup back, taking up the slack, and the car rights itself as the tyres regain the road.

The man unhitches the tow rope and comes back round to my window, brushing down his dusty green overalls. 'There you go. A bit muddy on the *derrière*, but no harm done.' He grins again, his dark eyes twinkling, and I'm not sure whether he's talking about me or my car. I restart my engine but he's still leaning in at the window, giving me an appraising look. In the midst of my confusion

47

and embarrassment, I register that he's really rather good-looking. Which only makes me blush even harder.

'Yes, well, thanks again.'

'It's my pleasure. Oh, *et bienvenue en France!*' He pats the roof of the car and steps back to let me pull away. I glance in my rear-view mirror just before I turn into the driveway and see that he's still standing in the lane, watching, before climbing back into his pickup and driving off. Almost as if he's seeing me safely home. Although more likely he's just having one last laugh at my expense.

I pull into the courtyard and turn off the engine, sitting for a few seconds with the realisation that I'm really here at last, and to allow both my embarrassment and the engine noise, which is still ringing in my ears, to subside.

It's early June, but feels like high summer already, and the leaves on the lime trees are a dense, dark green. As my hearing adjusts, I realise the sound in my ears is coming from their fresh-scented pale-yellow flowers, which are abuzz with bees in the golden warmth of the evening. The pots of pink geraniums by the kitchen door, which either Celia or Mireille must have put outside after their hibernation indoors over the winter, are dry and dusty.

I ease my stiff limbs out of the driver's seat, brushing as much mud off my jeans as possible, and dig in my handbag for the keys. Dragging my heavy suitcase and holdall from the boot, I unlock the kitchen door, pushing it open. And step into the cool half-light of my new home.

I wander through the house, opening shutters and windows, and the evening air floods in, the soundtrack of cicadas and bird-song exorcising the silence and emptiness that haunt the rooms.

In the quiet warmth of the summer's evening, I make my way upstairs to Liz's bedroom and hesitate before opening the door. The bed has been stripped and the duvet is folded neatly back over the end of the bedstead. I cross to the wardrobe and turn the key.

It's empty. Mireille has been true to her word and disposed of the rest of Liz's clothes. I pull on the cords that open the skylights and let the fresh air in and allow a couple of angrily buzzing flies to escape. I hadn't decided where I was going to sleep, but now I'm in here it seems more comforting, closer to Liz somehow, to make this my room.

I'm making my way back downstairs to fetch some sheets from the armoire that stands in the hall when I hear the crunch of footsteps in the gravel of the courtyard. Going into the kitchen, I find Lafite sitting looking at me expectantly. There's a gentle tap at the doorway and I turn to see Mireille standing on the threshold, a wicker basket on one arm and a bag in the other hand. Bending to put these down, she comes to embrace me warmly.

'*Ma chère* Gina, how good to see you've arrived safely,' she beams, her eyes crinkling in her wrinkled brown face. I look at her, a little surprised. I hadn't told anyone down here that I was coming. 'Aha,' she laughs, 'surely you didn't think your arrival would go unannounced and unnoticed? You are living in the country now, my dear, so you'll have to get used to everyone knowing your business even before you know it yourself! I heard from Madame Everett, who heard from your mother, that you would be arriving today. Lafite and I have been watching out for your car. No doubt Madame Everett will be round to call on you tomorrow, but I wanted to be the first to welcome you this evening.'

I wonder whether she witnessed my little encounter with the ditch and the good-looking Frenchman, but if she did she's too polite to mention it. She might know who he is though, so I make a mental note to ask her sometime.

She picks up the basket and bag and sets them on the kitchen table. 'Here are a few things to keep you going tonight and for your breakfast tomorrow, until you have a chance to get to the shops.' She takes a long loaf of crusty bread, some butter and a few eggs from the basket. 'And here are the very last of the cherries from my tree. The season's just over. There's a jar of my cherry jam too. And of course a bottle of wine to celebrate your homecoming. I'm so pleased you've decided to come and live here. Liz would have been delighted.

'Here are Lafite's things – his feeding dish, water bowl, some food. He's been happy with me, but I know he'll be even more pleased to be back where he belongs. He often pops back here to visit, you know – I think he's been waiting for you.'

'Mireille, you are so kind. Thank you. Will you stay and have a glass of wine?'

'Not today, my dear. I know you'll be tired after your long journey and want to get settled in. I'll leave you for now, but come and visit me whenever you wish. You know where I am if you need anything.'

With another hug, she picks up the empty basket and ambles off up the drive. Lafite winds himself about my ankles and then gazes up at my face, giving a plaintive-sounding meow.

'Supper time, is it? Come on then,' I say. 'And I think I'd better give those geraniums some water before they die of thirst.'

It's good to have some purposeful activities that need doing. I'd been dreading the silence and emptiness of my first evening here but now I bustle around, watering the pots in the courtyard, wiping dust off the kitchen surfaces, and making up the bed in Liz's room with crisply ironed sheets from the armoire that smell of fresh air, sunshine and lavender.

When I'm finished, I sigh, turning as if half expecting my aunt to be standing just behind me. This house is so full of her work and her character, her whole life contained within these old stone walls, which have become steeped with her presence. Perhaps that's what ghosts are, the essence of lives lived out that have become absorbed into the stonework and then radiated gently out again long after the people have gone, just as a stone wall will radiate the heat of the sun back into the evening air on a summer's night.

I pull myself together, reminding myself that I am, after all, my mother's daughter. What's happening to me? I've always been so self-controlled, but these days life seems to be shaking my foundations to the very core. Better have something to eat; it suddenly feels like a very long time since I stopped at a motorway service station for lunch.

I make some scrambled eggs and take my plate outside, with a glass of the wine that Mireille brought me, plopping down thankfully on to the bench on the terrace, bathed in evening light. Suddenly, I feel exhausted from the journey with its eventful ending in the ditch. I feel drained, too, from carrying the weight of grief for so long, and wrung out by all these memories that are still so vivid, replaying themselves with such clarity.

The last time I sat on this terrace was with Liz, and I think back to that last visit here. What a lot of endings, although I'd been so blissfully unaware at the time. We always know the first time we do anything, but we don't often know when it's our last time. Hindsight is a wonderful thing.

I take a sip of wine, holding up the glass to admire its colour in the last rays of evening sunshine. The bottle Mireille brought to welcome me to my new home is a Clairet, the local rosé. I remember helping Dad refill the bird feeder in our garden in the autumn, and hear him saying, 'Look at those bullfinches, Gina. A good rosé should be the same colour as their stomachs – precisely that gentle coral pink.' This wine is a bolder colour, more the orange-red of a robin's breast, and its chilled, dry complexity is thoroughly refreshing.

Lafite sits on the wall cleaning his whiskers and I suddenly feel a deep calm descend, the tension in my neck and shoulders relaxing as I watch the sky turn the same colour as the wine in my glass. The last swallows flit by, catching a few final flies in the warm evening air before slipping into their nests under the eaves for the night.

Despite my exhaustion at the end of such a long day, for the first time in a very, very long while I feel at peace. Now that I'm finally here in France, it feels as if I've been able to put down a heavy load that I've been carrying. The sorrow of loss, the pain of betrayal and the terror of an uncertain future are all still there, but they seem to recede a little in these new surroundings. And despite the fact that I'm so alone here, somehow I don't feel as lonely and abandoned as I did back in England. Perhaps I'm going to enjoy rural life.

In the oak trees, an owl hoots gently.

I raise my glass. 'Thank you, Liz,' I whisper.

Chapter 6

Time goes by, as Madonna observed in one of her more philosophical moments, so slowly. Especially when it's two in the morning and the prospect of sleep has become as unlikely as the prospect of a reliable man or a steady job. Despite the fact that I'm exhausted after the long drive, I toss and turn all night, my mind abuzz with a jumble of thoughts and memories in the unfamiliar darkness of Liz's bedroom. I'm a fully paid-up, card-carrying insomniac these days.

Dawn is just breaking when I reach for my notebook to write my to-do list for the day, but then Lafite shoulders the bedroom door open and jumps up on to the bed, meowing enquiringly. I stroke his wise old head. 'Quite right! That's enough lying around; we've got things to do. Starting with breakfast for you, I know.'

A couple of hours later, I'm sitting at the desk in Liz's study – my study, I mean – the reality of my new situation slowly sinking in. I've been speaking to the phone company and feel a huge sense of achievement and relief as I've managed to negotiate the tortuous push-button system (frequently pressing the button to '*répéter les options*' as I strain to understand the alternatives being offered me in rapid-fire French) and am assured by the real human being I finally managed to speak to that my internet connection will be up and running in a week's time.

I jump slightly at the sound of tyres on the gravel outside. Looking at my watch, I smile. Ten thirty. This must be Celia coming to check up on me. She hasn't wasted much time. I thought she'd consider afternoon tea a more socially acceptable point at which to call. But then, looking out of the window, I see a huge cream-coloured Mercedes cruise into the courtyard like an ocean liner, dwarfing my little car as it docks in the shade of the lime trees.

As I watch, a dapper middle-aged man steps out, wearing a pair of trousers that would be described in the ads at the back of the *Daily Telegraph* as 'permapress slacks', and a navy blazer with two rows of glittering gold buttons down the front. He pauses to look up appraisingly at the façade of the house and then smooths back his suspiciously shiny hair at either temple. He walks briskly to the front door and knocks on it with three confidently sharp raps.

Flustered, I hesitate, ruefully aware of the fact that this morning I pulled on the first clothes that came to hand from the top of my holdall. I'm dressed, somewhat skimpily, for a morning of unpacking, cleaning, weeding the woefully neglected garden and, most importantly, a little sitting in the sun in between it all, in a halter-neck top and a pair of worn jeans that I now deeply regret cutting off at upper-thigh level last summer. It's a look that's definitely more Daisy Duke than Doris Day.

Can I pretend I'm not here? But to my horror, the man is now opening the door and he sticks his head through to call, "'Allo. Ees zere anybodee zere?'

I draw myself up to my full five foot six, tall enough to look most Frenchmen in the eye, and march out of the study to confront him.

'*Bonjour*, Monsieur,' I say, hoping the iciness of my tone will freeze his overconfidence. But not a bit of it. With a broad smile, which displays two rows of yellowing teeth, he steps across the threshold to shake my hand. I try not to blush as he gives my outfit an appraising glance, but feel my cheeks flush with embarrassment as he grins, seeming to enjoy my discomfort.

'Mademoiselle. Please excuse this intrusion,' he says in heavily accented English. 'I am Laurent Dubois. I 'ave come to welcome you to the region and to extend my sympathies to you for the sad loss of your aunt.' His cheerful smile and jaunty tone suggest that this sadness is somewhat less than heartfelt.

'*Merci, Monsieur Dubois, vous êtes très gentil,*' I reply, continuing firmly in French. 'Do you live nearby?' His name is ringing a faint bell, but I can't quite place him.

'In Sainte-Foy,' comes the reply, again in English. 'I 'ave known your aunt for many years.'

Suddenly the penny drops. '*Ah, oui*, Dubois Immobilier in the rue Marceau.'

Of course. In the plate-glass window, among the details of properties for sale, there's a large photo displaying the same slicked-back hair and toothy smile and beneath this the words 'English spoken'.

With a flourish, he pulls a business card from the breast pocket of his blazer. 'At your service, Mademoiselle. If you are wishing to sell this property, I 'ave a client who might be interested in buying it. Of course, you would need to do some work on it first. The paintwork needs redoing and you may wish to consider replacing the windows with plastic frames, which are so much more desirable. The roof needs some work on it as well. I can give you the telephone number of my brother-in-law 'oo is in the building trade, if you wish.'

I'm a little startled at the directness of his approach, to say the least, and feel my face flushing again, this time with annoyance rather than embarrassment. 'That's very kind of you, but I'm not selling at the moment.'

'I also 'andle rentals. Although you will still 'ave to do the repairs to get the 'ouse into a better condition. There are not many English renting long term at the moment. And without a swimming pool, it will be 'ard to get 'oliday rentals.'

'*Merci*,' I reply, firmly persisting with my French. It's starting to feel like a competition to see who will submit first linguistically, and I'm damned if I'm going to be the one to give in. 'But I'm not renting it out either. I'm going to live here.'

Laurent Dubois looks me up and down approvingly once again and this time his gaze is, frankly, lascivious. '*Bravo*, Mademoiselle, that is good news for our little corner of the world. And you will still need the services of my brother-in-law no doubt. But per'aps I can be of assistance in 'andling the necessary works for you.' As if to demonstrate his 'andling skills here and now, he pauses to place a slightly damp hand on my bare arm, just a little too near the cotton of my halter-neck top, which suddenly feels dangerously flimsy.

I look down at his hand with what I hope is eloquent disdain, but he doesn't remove it. Okay, no more Mrs Nice Guy. I take his sticky paw between thumb and forefinger and firmly remove it, raising my eyebrows and looking pointedly at his gold wedding ring. '*Vraiment, Monsieur Dubois*, I assure you I have no need of the services of either you or your brother-in-law, nor anyone else just at present. My aunt lived in this house for over thirty years and if it was okay for her, it's okay for me. Now, thank you for your visit, but if you'll excuse me, I have work to do. My regards to Madame Dubois. *Au revoir*.' And I usher him firmly out of the door.

The estate agent, apparently unabashed, grins at me. But his final retort is in French, so I congratulate myself on winning that battle at least. '*Ah, les Anglaises*. Always with a closed mind. You don't understand how pleasant our little French ways can be. And I assure you,' he finishes with an upward glance, 'you'll regret not seeing to that roof. Welcome to the region, Mademoiselle.'

And with a jaunty mock salute he climbs back into his cruise ship of a car and sails off, with unhurried insouciance, down the drive.

'Bloody cheek,' I mutter, going back inside. Another cheating slime-bag. There seem to be a lot of them about these days.

I sit down at the desk, but there's not much I can do with no proper internet for another week. The phone reception about these parts is decidedly sketchy. I think back to the last time I saw Liz sitting here in the study, surrounded by the remnants of her life's work, and suddenly feel overwhelmed with sadness again. Quickly shaking it off, I go outside and find a few jobs to do in the garden to keep myself busy, taking out my anger on the weeds at the cheek of the estate agent.

◆ ◆ ◆

That night I lie awake as usual. The moon isn't helping my sleepless state either. It must be almost full. I've left the blinds open and its white light streams in through the windows in the roof, illuminating the room as clearly as one of Liz's black-and-white prints. With a flicker of annoyance as I recall the estate agent's damp hand on my bare arm, I turn restlessly on to my side, trying to find a more relaxing position, and hopefully one in which sleep may be possible. The hot, still air clings damply to my skin and I throw off the thin cotton sheet, trying to find a cooler part of the bed.

Reaching for my watch on the bedside table, my gaze falls on the photo in the heavy silver frame. Six magpies in a tree, their black tails outlined clearly against a white sky.

And then, my detached mind registering the fact almost dreamily, I realise there is one more. Sitting within the cross-hatch of the branches, its straight tail feathers look like just another twig.

But there, above the tail, is the unmistakable rounded bulk of the bird's body and head.

I sit bolt upright in the bed. I hear Liz's voice again, clear as a bell, and remember how she'd turned away as she said, 'Ah, seven. Seven for a secret never to be told.'

Even as I turn the frame over and ease back the clips that have rusted slightly into the velvet backing, I'm telling myself not to be silly. There won't be anything here. It's just a photo of a few birds, not some melodramatic message from beyond the grave.

In the moonlight, I prise a sheet of thick photographic paper from the frame.

And then suddenly I'm looking into my father's eyes.

They are smiling with a loving, tender gaze, right into the camera, as he leans forward, lips parted, to say something to the person taking the picture. Across one corner of the print, in his handwriting that is as familiar to me as my own, is a message. It reads, 'For Liz – my love, always, David.'

As if the look in his dark, moonlit eyes hadn't already said it all.

Chapter 7

Oh. My. God.

As every insomniac knows, there's a kind of madness that comes with the night. The connections in the brain, which in the light of day allow it to function quite rationally, somehow become scrambled. The normally unthinkable becomes perfectly possible, if not probable. The doubts and fears, banished in daylight to dark corners, come creeping out and push any sensible thoughts away into some unreachable chasm.

Tonight, any chance of sleep makes its escape out of the skylights above my head, the way lit by stark white moonbeams.

At first I try to come up with a sensible, rational explanation for the photo of my father. Perhaps it's just someone who looks like him. (But it's definitely him – and, anyway, it's his writing and he's signed his name.) Perhaps it was a photo meant for my mother. (But it's inscribed to Liz.) Perhaps it's just a token of friendship. ('My love, always'? The look in his eyes?) Perhaps it's a forgotten memento from an affair before he met my mother. (Still in a silver frame beside Liz's bed?)

I rack my brains for snippets of family history that might help me date the picture. Liz wasn't at my parents' wedding: that I know from photos in a heavy old cream leather album, embossed at the corners with overlapping gold lines, which I used to love to pore over when I was little. I once asked Mum why Liz wasn't among the small crowd of guests posing on the registry office steps and she said her sister had been working in New York at the time and that transatlantic travel wasn't nearly as easy, nor as cheap, as it is nowadays. According to Mum, Dad had swept her off her feet and asked her to marry him just a couple of months after they'd met at an exhibition in London. 'She was the most beautiful girl in the room,' my father had chimed in with a fond smile. 'I can still remember the dress she was wearing, and she had her hair pinned up in a most becoming style.'

As far as I know, my father didn't meet his sister-in-law until after he and Mum were married.

I pick up the photo and look at it again, bracing myself for the pang of pain and betrayal I know I'll feel. I turn on the bedside lamp to look at the image more clearly, the familiar, well-loved features seeming like those of a stranger in this bewildering new context.

His face is young and fresh, the photo taken years before lines etched themselves across his forehead and grey hairs eroded the dark sand of the hair at his temples. This same face gazes out from pages and pages of pictures in the cream leather album. Engagement photos. Wedding photos. Photos of him cradling his newborn baby daughter in his arms. Him and Mum. Him and me.

I put the picture back, face down, on the bedside table and reach over to turn off the light. On second thoughts, I think I'll leave it on, so that the dark shadows that threaten to crowd in on me as the moon continues on its way across the starlit sky will be kept pinned back against the walls, where they belong. I turn over, trying to find a cooler patch of pillow to cushion my burning cheek and my overheated brain.

And then the crazily jumbled thoughts in my head say, 'What if Liz is really my mother, but in some strange twist of events she gave me to her younger sister?' I hear an echo of Ed's voice saying, 'You were just like a daughter to the old girl.'

But in my mind's eye I can see, as clearly as if it were beside me on the bedside table too, another photo from the same old album. Mum lying back in a hospital bed, propped up against crisp white pillows, with a small bundle tightly wrapped in a pink honeycomb blanket, held carefully in her arms. Her hair, usually immaculately set, is dishevelled, and on her exhausted face are written pain and love in equal quantities. 'It was such a difficult labour,' she'd said. 'In the end they had to do an emergency caesarean. So it was no more bikinis for me from then on.'

As the long night wears on and the pool of yellow light from the bedside lamp starts to dissolve into the paleness of dawn, the whirl of thoughts slows and then comes to a silent stop.

And then, all other possibilities exhausted, I'm left with the certain knowledge that my father and my aunt, two of the people I have trusted and loved most dearly in my life, have betrayed my mother and me with a secret love of their own.

◆ ◆ ◆

Now I'm angry. I'm angry with Dad and with Liz for obvious reasons. I'm angry, too, because they've both gone and left me alone with the fact of their affair but no way of getting the further explanation that they owe me. I'm angry with my mother, and I'm not quite sure why. If she'd been a bit warmer towards my father, maybe things would have been different. Did her coolness drive him into Liz's arms? And, above all, I'm absolutely furious with myself for being so naive as to believe that anyone on this godforsaken planet could ever be faithful. I feel betrayed by everybody I've ever trusted, as though what seemed to be solid ground has turned into quicksand beneath my feet.

My anger gives me a surge of energy and I get up and dress briskly. Then I clatter downstairs to Liz's study, Lafite giving me a look of baleful reproach as he flees before me.

I pull open drawer after drawer in her desk and filing cabinets, searching for letters, diaries, anything that will expose what really happened between her and Dad. But she's done a thorough job of clearing everything out – I think again, coldly this time, of those black bin bags – and there's nothing much left. I race back up the stairs, taking them two at a time, to the bedroom and wrench open chests and cupboards. Again nothing, except for the neatly folded sheets of brown paper that line the shelves and drawers. I lift these up but beneath them is just the dusty wood, scattered with a few dried grains of faintly scented lavender.

I turn to the photos lying on the bedside table. Picking them up, I go back downstairs, moving more calmly this time, and into the kitchen. Lafite is sitting patiently by his dish and looks up serenely as I enter. I put the photos carefully on the kitchen table and come over, chastened, to stroke his broad old head. 'Sorry. Did I scare you earlier? None of this is your fault, you poor old boy. I wish you could tell me what you know, though.' He slowly blinks his eyes in forgiveness, given that it looks as though breakfast is imminent, and I pour food into his chipped bowl.

As I drink my coffee and spread cherry jam on a hunk of slightly stale bread, I look at the two photos on the table beside my plate. The light of day brings new clarity, the irrational tumble of night-time thoughts banished, like vampires, at least until darkness falls again.

It strikes me that there are three alternatives here.

The first is that Liz meant to 'clear away' the photo before she died, as she had methodically tidied away the rest of her life, but had hung on to it and then been taken sooner than she'd expected. It's a distinct possibility.

The second is that she never meant the photo to be discovered beneath the picture of the magpies, which seems unlikely and risky.

And the third, which dawns on me as clearly as the bright sunshine that is now streaming in through the window as I chew a mouthful of crust, almost unconsciously savouring the sweet tartness of the black cherries, is that she meant me to find it. That in fact it is a message to me from beyond the grave. But why not just put it in an envelope addressed with my name?

Because it's still a secret never to be told. But perhaps Liz wants me to know, now that both she and Dad are gone.

And maybe the person she wants to protect by keeping the secret is not her niece, but her sister.

◆ ◆ ◆

When the going gets tough, the tough get cleaning. I suppose it's a way of trying to impose some sense of control when every other area of my life has collapsed into uncertainty and disarray. Two days after discovering the hidden photo, I'm still awaiting the arrival of the France Télécom engineer to sort out my internet connection and I need to do something to distract myself from the thoughts, threatening to verge on the unhealthily obsessive now, that go round and round in my head. Like a hamster running desperately on a wheel in its cage, I'm getting nowhere fast.

Cleaning is a good way of using up the angry energy that's fizzing in my veins, refusing to allow me to settle down peacefully with a good book. And, if I'm honest, there's always the possibility that I might uncover some more bits of the jigsaw and begin to piece together exactly what went on between Liz and Dad. So I set to work methodically, room by room, scrubbing, dusting, polishing. I even open up and clean the sitting room (scarcely used) and dining room (never used), moving the ancient, solid pieces of furniture to vacuum beneath them and sending long-undisturbed spiders scuttling frantically for new cover. Other than dust and cobwebs, I find nothing.

When I've finished cleaning, I start washing. Perhaps I'm trying to wipe the slate clean so that I can live in a state of happy denial and transform my family history back into the neat storybook facsimile it used to be. I wash bedding and cushions and chair covers, hanging them to dry on the line stretched between two apple trees in the garden. The turnaround is gratifyingly fast in the hot sun so I work unremittingly, dragging load after load out of the machine, carrying armfuls of dry, sun-warmed fabric from the line back into the kitchen and sweating over the ironing board, where clouds of hissing, angry steam from the iron create the perfect backing track to my mood.

After several days of this frenetic activity, I smooth the freshly laundered *toile de Jouy* bedspread over the mattress in the spare room and stand back to survey my handiwork. There's nothing else to wash or dust or polish. I regret the fact that there are no curtains at the windows, which would have kept me going for a few more days, other than the small ones under the eaves in the bedroom upstairs that I laundered yesterday. I move to the window to close the shutters against the midday heat that's now building to a stifling crescendo of sun glare and cricket song, the humidity making my T-shirt cling limply to my clammy skin.

Triumphantly, I realise that here's my next project. The shutters are in dire need of a fresh coat of paint. Their sun-cracked red finish has faded to a drab brown tinge, like a bottle of old wine that's gone past the point of drinkability. While I'm at it, I think I'll change the colour completely. Make my mark on the house. And – yes, I know – symbolically try to blot out a bit more of the past. It's called catharsis, isn't it?

I jump into the car and arrive at the DIY centre, Mr. Bricolage, just as they're locking the doors. Of course, it's noon and every shop and business in the area is now closing for a two-hour lunch break. Only in France . . .

At two o'clock precisely, I'm back in Mr. Bricolage's car park, waiting for the doors to open. I choose a sage-green gloss and a selection of brushes, congratulating myself on remembering to add a large bottle of brush cleaner to my basket. I've never attempted any DIY before, but, after all, it's not exactly rocket science.

Back at the house, I haul a stepladder out of the shed and drag it across the courtyard to the first set of shutters. It's a good thing only the ground-floor windows have them, so I don't have to climb too high. This should be a doddle.

I dip a large brush into the can of pale green paint and begin spreading it over the rusty red. How very satisfying. My soft sage colour spreads easily over the cracked, blistered surface, erasing the old and the worn with a beautiful shiny covering. Of course, it's still a bit uneven, but that's good, I tell myself – it looks more weathered and rustic. I wouldn't have wanted to make the shutters look too new. Quite a lot of paint is dripping on to the ground below, so I spread a couple of bin bags below the ladder. And somehow quite a lot of paint is also getting itself on to the handle of the brush and running down the sides of the tin. And then dripping on to the steps of the ladder and, inexplicably, transferring itself from there to my arms, legs and hair. Good job I remembered the cleaning fluid or I'd look like a soldier in full camouflage gear.

It's a fiddly job trying to paint the ironwork catches and the hinges, and quite a lot of paint also manages to get itself on to the stonework. I go to fetch some cleaning things and discover I've left a trail of sage-green footprints across the recently scrubbed kitchen floor. It's not easy to get gloss paint off stonework either, I find, and my attempts just seem to smear it into a series of bigger stains. I'm starting to get a bit fed up with this job. But I've only painted one pair of shutters and there are . . . I tally them up in my head . . . another six sets to do, so twelve more. Oh, plus the big set on the kitchen door. And the terrace door. And the main door. So that's an additional six, which are twice the size. Oh, God, I wish I'd never started this. And I'm going to need to go and get more paint tomorrow too.

My manic burst of energy seems suddenly depleted and I feel exhausted and overwhelmed with a sense of hopelessness at the task ahead of me. But I know I'm going to need to keep going or else I'll drown in the thoughts of despair and betrayal that crash over me like an ocean wave whenever I stop. I put the ladder away and stick my brushes into an old ice-cream tub to soak. I pause to look at my day's handiwork. From across the courtyard, the spare-room shutters don't look bad at all. In fact, they really look quite elegant. And in the fading light you can hardly see the blobs of paint on the walls around them.

◆ ◆ ◆

That night I collapse into bed after a lukewarm bath to try to take the edge off the now oppressive heat. I've used a nail brush and half a bottle of orange blossom body wash to try to remove the paint from my skin.

I must have successfully worn myself out, because I fall into a deep, muggy sleep straight away, drugged by the humid night air, which is as heavy as a thick woollen blanket.

I'm woken a few hours later by the needling whine of a mosquito. I pull the sheet, the only covering on the bed tonight, over my head. But it's suffocatingly hot like that, so after a few minutes I emerge again. I've left the skylights open to try to get a bit of air into the room and at last, thankfully, I feel the gentle caress of a cool night breeze. I sigh with relief. Now hopefully the mosquito will leave too and there's a chance I'll be able to get back to sleep. I let myself drift off, noting with pleasure the slight ache in my arms and down the back of my calves from today's physical activities. Just relax and sleep will come . . .

Suddenly, there's the most almighty flash of light, blinding even through closed eyelids, and simultaneously a sharp, ear-splitting crack as though some giant axe has split the house in two. My heart leaps against the wall of my ribcage and for a second I think I'm having a cardiac arrest, but the fact that it's now pounding like the pistons on a steam train tells me that it's still working, pumping a massive surge of adrenaline through my veins, definitely inspiring flight rather than fight. I wrench the sheet over my head again, as if a thin piece of cotton is going to protect me from the cacophony that's erupted in the sky above, as the violent thunderstorm, which I now realise has been brewing for the last few oppressive, overheated days, suddenly explodes directly overhead.

A rush of wind whips the sheet out of my shaking grip and icy drops of hard rain pelt my skin. I leap up, gasping with panic and the chill of the raindrops. I grab the pole to yank shut the skylights, hoping desperately that it won't act as a lightning conductor and leave me lying in a frizzled heap on the floor.

The wind swirls, the rain is a deafening roar and the thunder and lightning rage. I grab a top and a pair of jeans off a chair and make my way downstairs, feeling I'll be a little safer there than upstairs with only the roof between me and the storm. When I get to the kitchen door I flick on the light switch and spot Lafite cowering under the table, his fur spiky from the rain. I get down on my hands and knees and crawl in to join him. I'm only trying to comfort him, honest, I tell myself. I'm not really hiding from a thunderstorm underneath a kitchen table at the age of nearly thirty, for heaven's sake. And then there's another almighty crash, which makes the whole house shake and the lights go out. It's completely black, partly because I'm still under the tent of the (freshly washed and ironed) tablecloth and partly because the storm seems to have discharged its entire supply of thunder and lightning with that last blow. So I sit on the floor under the table in the pitch darkness, stroking Lafite and listening to the pouring rain drumming on the roof above us.

◆ ◆ ◆

The next morning, the sky is a fresh blue, as clear and innocent as the wide eyes of a child. 'Storm – what storm?' it seems to say.

I emerge a little creakily from beneath the kitchen table, where I've spent an uncomfortable night, terrified that the distant rumbles of thunder and flickers of lightning might swing back this way again. I must have fallen asleep, with Lafite curled up on the floor beside me, once the night fell silent again.

The air is refreshingly cool and I go outside into the courtyard to review the damage. To my relief, everything looks okay. And then I spot my lovely green shutters. They appear to have developed some sort of hideous skin problem. Patches of paint are now lifting off like scales, exposing bare wood underneath. Closer inspection shows that last night's rain has made the most of this opportunity and thoroughly soaked the old panels. I prod a brown patch tentatively with a fingernail and it's as soft as damp cardboard. And in the places where the sun is drying out the soaking wood, the paint is splitting and peeling almost before my eyes. Oh, God, what a disaster.

But it's nothing like the disaster that is waiting for me round the other side of the house, where one of the tall stone chimney stacks has fallen, taking a large section of moss-covered roof tiles with it as it crashed to the terrace below.

There's a gaping hole in the roof and I dash back inside and upstairs to the bedroom. Through jagged wooden teeth, the ceiling gapes open to the sky. Bits of broken plaster are scattered across the damp bed, washed up in a tide of fine dust. And in the middle of the floor sits the heavy concrete cowl from the top of the chimney. The oily estate agent's ominous prediction about the state of the roof comes back to haunt me.

I run down to the study and pick up the phone, hands shaking as I leaf through my address book to find Hugh and Celia's number. But the line is dead and I realise that the power is still off and without it the phone won't work. I run back upstairs and retrieve my handbag from the debris to try my mobile phone. Damn, I haven't charged it for days and now the battery's dead. Well, I'll just have to get in the car and drive over to the Everetts'.

But as I round the curve of the drive, the landscape looks strangely unfamiliar. It takes me a couple of shocked seconds to register that one of the tall oaks has been blown over and is now blocking my exit. So I'm stuck. Completely and utterly cut off. And completely and utterly alone. I have to admit that my British stiff upper lip is beginning to feel decidedly wobbly now, in the face of these natural disasters on top of the man-made ones that have been inflicted upon me of late.

But suddenly I notice that I'm not completely alone and in fact rescue is at hand. Making her way purposefully along the lane is a little old lady in a familiar black dress and now she's waving reassuringly at me and shouting something I can't quite hear.

With a surge of relief and gratitude, I jump out of the car and clamber over the tangled branches of the fallen tree to hug Mireille, my saviour.

When I lead her on to the terrace, she tuts sympathetically at the scene of devastation before her. 'My dear girl, it's so lucky you weren't hurt. Now, don't worry about a thing. The electricity will be back on soon. They're used to these storms around here and I saw the EDF van going past a few minutes ago.'

I sigh deeply. 'Well, once the phones are back on, I suppose I'll have to call Monsieur Dubois and ask him for his brother-in-law's number so I can get him to come round and mend the roof.'

'Pah,' retorts Mireille with utter scorn. 'That philandering Parisian. You're not having any of *them* to do the work. No, you have the perfect workforce much closer at hand. Don't you know my sons are stonemasons? They'll come round and sort all this out for you. And I'll tell Raphael to bring the chainsaw, too, so they can clear your driveway before they do anything else.'

Weak-kneed with relief, I sit down on the terrace wall. 'Oh, Mireille, I'd be so grateful. But it's the weekend. I can probably manage until Monday if they wouldn't mind coming then.'

'Weekend nothing! In an emergency we all lend a hand to help our neighbours in the country, you know. They'll be here this afternoon. I'm the boss!' And with a final reassuring pat on my tousled head, she sweeps regally back up the lane to mobilise her troops.

◆ ◆ ◆

At precisely two o'clock, I hear the purposeful hum of a distant chainsaw at the foot of the drive. Mireille taps at the kitchen door. 'They're just clearing the tree so they can get the truck through. Have you got your power back on? Good. They'll leave the trunk lying in the grass. You'll have a good supply of wood for the fire, but oak is tough so it needs to season for a year before you can cut it up. At least it'll be out of your way, though. Ah, here they come now.'

A large white truck rumbles ponderously up the drive and sways to a halt in the courtyard, dwarfing my little car. On the side is stencilled '*Thibault Frères, Maçonnerie*' and a local phone number.

Two smiling men jump out and are followed by two more on foot, one of them carrying a large orange chainsaw.

And, to my horror and surprise, I realise that the one with the chainsaw is none other than Blue Pickup Guy. He gives me a somewhat cheeky grin, leading me to suspect that he must have known exactly who I was the other day.

All four of them are wearing neat green overalls and they line up respectfully before their mother, towering above her, awaiting her instructions.

'Mademoiselle Gina, these are my sons,' she says with a hint of maternal pride. 'Raphael, Florian, Cédric and Pierre. Of course, I think you've already met Cédric.' Her expression gives nothing away, but I imagine they've had a good laugh at my expense over my Close Encounter of the Muddy Kind the other day.

Each in turn reaches to shake my hand. The first three have warm, dark eyes the colour of molasses and neat brush-cut hair, graded from salt-and-pepper (Raphael), through greying at the temples (Florian) to pure black (Cédric, aka Mr Pickup; he's just as good-looking as he was the other day, especially sporting the lumberjack look with chainsaw in hand).

The fourth, Pierre, who appears to be a good few years younger than the others, has an unruly mop of dark curls and blue eyes that sparkle with self-confident charm.

'It's a great pleasure to meet you,' I say. 'And thank you for coming to help me so quickly.' I repeat each of their names in turn to make sure I've got them right.

'Pierre?' I say with a smile, as a thought occurs to me – it's the French word for 'stone'. It reminds me of those old jokes – what do you call a man with a seagull on his head? Cliff. A stonemason called Pierre is like a miner called Doug. Or a gardener called Flora. Or a DJ called Mike (although, come to think of it, I'm sure there've been quite a few of those). It's obviously a well-worn joke, as Pierre rolls his eyes and his three brothers grin.

'Yes, I know,' sighs Mireille. 'My dear departed husband, may God rest his soul, was a stonemason. When his first son was born he wanted to call him Pierre. But I had other ideas. It was the same with Florian and Cédric. Finally, when we knew another baby was on the way, several years after Cédric, I was absolutely sure it was going to be a girl this time. So to keep my husband happy, I said if it was a boy we could call him Pierre. And so here he is.'

'Although some would say he *is* a bit of a girl, with this head of hair,' teases Florian, ruffling his baby brother's head to annoy him.

'Ah, you're just jealous because I'm so popular with the women,' shrugs Pierre. Cédric rolls his eyes in mock despair and grins at me and I notice that around his smiling eyes is an etching of finely chiselled lines that seem to tell a story of something else: weariness or sadness or pain? Whatever it is, it runs beneath the surface like a deeply buried fault line through bedrock. It's intriguing, and only serves to increase his handsomely rugged appearance.

'That's enough, boys,' says their mother firmly. 'Come and see what needs to be done round the other side of the house.' She and I lead the way. The four men take the scene of devastation completely in their stride and quickly set to work like a well-oiled machine, each getting on with his own tasks.

'Don't worry, Gina, they'll soon have this put right. At the very least you'll have the hole in the roof patched up before nightfall,' says Mireille comfortingly.

They are putting up a scaffolding tower beside the house and Cédric is surveying the roof from the top of a tall ladder alongside it. 'There's quite a bit of damage to the tiles up here,' he calls down. 'Really, the whole roof needs to be redone. Some of these joists look like they need replacing completely.'

With dismay I think of my redundancy money, which won't go far if it has to pay for a whole new roof. I wonder what the insurance will cover. Seeing the look on my face, Mireille says, 'Well, just patch it up as best you can for now. If Gina decides she wants the whole thing done later, you can always come back.' She turns to me. 'I'm going to leave you now. Nathalie and her brother Luc are at my house for the afternoon so I'd better get back. Just ask the boys if you have any questions or need any help.'

I hug her and thank her profusely for saving me.

'Nonsense – that's what neighbours are for,' she replies.

A couple of hours later, I stick my head out of the French windows. 'Would anyone like a cup of tea?' I ask.

'*Non merci*,' reply Raphael and Florian, with looks of alarm at the thought of this strange foreign idea. But Cédric says, 'Please, I'd like to try one,' and Pierre says, 'A coffee would be good for me,' so I busy myself setting things out on a tray.

'It's so kind of you, coming to help me out on a Saturday,' I say as the two younger brothers pause with their drinks.

'It's no problem,' smiles Cédric kindly, gingerly sipping a cup of black tea. 'We'll fix things up temporarily today and come back next week to finish the job properly.' The floral cup looks delicate in his large, capable hand. I can't help noticing again how good-looking he is, his features strongly chiselled, alight with a warmth that speaks of a lively sense of humour behind the professional façade. I find myself drawn to him, despite our inauspicious first meeting. He's a little quieter than the others, a bit reserved, and seems to hold himself at a slight distance from their easy bantering. And yet there's a kindness in his expression and an air of thoughtfulness as he listens carefully to my responses to his questions about how I'm finding life in France.

Pierre, meanwhile, has knocked back his coffee in a single gulp and is busily consulting the mobile phone he's fished out of a pocket of his overalls.

'Aha,' says Cédric, 'Pierre is busy fixing up his social life for this evening. He's usually spoilt for choice on a Saturday night.'

Contemplating the blankness of my own social diary, I mean to express the fact that I'm envious of Pierre's dilemma. '*Ah, j'ai envie de toi,*' I say.

And then, given the look of surprise on the faces of both men, I realise I've just come out with one of those awful linguistic mistakes that still ambush me every now and then, even though I definitely should know better.

Cédric throws back his head and guffaws. 'Mademoiselle Gina, I think you mean to say, "*Je t'envie*"!'

Oh God, I feel myself blushing to the roots of my hair as it dawns on me that I've just told Mireille's youngest son that I desire him.

Pierre, in the meantime, has regained his composure and replies, with a studied air of nonchalance, 'Well, perhaps she *does* mean what she says. It's a common reaction among women when they first meet me, after all.'

Cédric gives him a mock cuff around the ear. 'Insufferable brat,' he says fondly. 'Just ignore him,' he tells me.

In confusion, I collect our cups and scurry back inside, blushing again as I hear Pierre recounting my mistake to his two elder brothers on the roof, who both whoop with laughter.

By five thirty, they've patched the hole in the roof with plastic sheeting and have made a neat stack of unbroken roof tiles, clearing away the shattered debris. 'If they're not in your way, we'll leave our tools here until Monday,' says Raphael, and I assure him I'm not planning on carrying out any major terrace renovations myself this weekend. They take their leave and the truck swings up the drive, Raphael and Florian in the front and the two younger men perched in the back.

I follow on foot to go and check whether there's any post in the metal box on the lane. I reach into the box and pull out a large envelope with a coloured crest and 'Institute of Masters of Wine' inscribed in one corner. My spirits lift. It's the confirmation that I've been accepted on to the course.

I look up as I hear a roar in the lane, and a cavalcade of vehicles pulls out of Mireille's gate. First comes a helmeted figure on a red motorbike, who sweeps by with a jaunty wave – Pierre, I surmise, heading off for his Saturday night social whirl. Next, a stately green Volvo sails by and Raphael gives me a grave salute. Then the white truck comes past and Florian waves at me cheerfully. And finally, the familiar dark-blue pickup comes along the lane with Cédric at the wheel. Next to him is a young boy with the same dark hair and eyes as his father. And from the narrow back seat, a serious, heart-shaped face framed with long dark hair gazes out.

Of course. I should have known. I manage a smile, but my heart feels as if it's just tumbled into the dust beneath my feet. He's married.

They pull up alongside and Nathalie winds down her window. '*Bonjour*, Mam'selle Gina. Was Lafite all right in the storm? I hope he wasn't too frightened.'

'Hello, Nathalie. Don't worry, he's fine. I think I was more afraid than he was. He didn't much like getting his fur wet, though.'

'Give him a stroke from me,' she replies.

'I will. You'll have to come and see him one day soon. He's missing you.'

The little girl smiles and Cédric pulls off with a wave. I stand by the postbox, watching them disappear up the road.

And am surprised to note that I feel a distinctly painful pang of disappointment at the realisation that Nathalie and Luc belong to Cédric, and not to Florian or Raphael.

Chapter 8

The next morning, determined not to be beaten by my disastrous first attempt at painting and decorating, I put on my cut-off shorts and a vest top that has definitely seen better days, and stand, hands on hips, surveying the scabrous, flaking shutters. Sunday is cranking itself up to be another baking-hot day and so at least the soft old wood has dried out now. The peeling patches of paint are worse than ever, though, and there's no doubt it all needs to be removed somehow. I'm sure I saw some sheets of sandpaper in a drawer in the kitchen during my frantic cleaning frenzy and I go in search of them and also my phone, which I tuck into the back pocket of my shorts, fixing the earbuds into my ears. A little energising music is just what I need for this job.

Now, we might as well get this out into the open up front: I freely confess my taste in music is not always the coolest. Stashed away in a playlist cunningly entitled 'Classics' is my shameful secret library. Meat Loaf, Cher and Bonnie Tyler rub shoulders with Kirsty MacColl, The Bangles and Dixie Chicks. Bryan Adams and Enrique Iglesias compete with Take That and Boyzone for my attention. And Plastic Bertrand and Johnny Hallyday add a little French culture – if 'culture' is the right word, which it probably isn't.

Oh, come on, there's a time and a place for Mozart – and sanding shutters definitely isn't it. And anyway, let he or she who is entirely without an Abba number tucked away somewhere in their collection cast the first stone.

So now I select my secret playlist, crank up the volume and set to with the sandpaper. The paint, both old and new, comes off with gratifying ease. It's good exercise too, especially if you add a few dance moves while you work, although the stepladder does tend to wobble a bit. My spirits lift as a new, smoothly uniform surface of freshly sanded wood is exposed, and I start to sing along to *Que je t'aime*.

I'm duetting with Johnny Hallyday – telling him in no uncertain terms, as the song reaches its climax, that when it's me saying *non* and him saying *oui*, oh how I love him – when suddenly I realise there's someone else standing there watching me.

Luckily, he's close enough to put a steadying hand on the stepladder, as I jump so hard it lurches alarmingly. I look down from my precarious perch into the bemused face of Cédric.

Wrenching the earbuds from my ears, I scramble down to firmer ground, my neck and cheeks blazing scarlet with embarrassment. 'Excuse me, I was just . . .' I burble, waving a dusty hand at the shutters. My shoulders and arms are covered in freckles of dried green and red paint. And it's only later that I discover the bits in my hair as well.

Why is it that whenever I'm wearing my most scruffy and revealing clothes, an unexpected Frenchman comes sailing up the drive? Perhaps there's a whole posse of them lurking in the bushes watching and then the minute I put on an outfit that I'd prefer not to be seen dead in, they send another one along to ensure maximum mortification. I can just imagine Monsieur Dubois nudging Cédric, 'Go on, I did it last time. Your turn next . . .'

And exactly how long has he been standing there? I cast my mind back to the previous song on the playlist. Omigod, did he get here in time to catch my ladder-top rendition of 'There's a guy works down the chip shop swears he's Elvis'?

Cédric gallantly pretends he hasn't noticed that I'm not really wearing many clothes, nor that he's witnessed any of my grand command performance up the ladder. Composing his features into an expression of professional gravity (though that irrepressible twinkle in his eyes speaks volumes), he shakes my grubby hand.

I try hard not to notice all over again how gorgeous he is.

'*Bonjour*, Mademoiselle Gina. Please forgive me for disturbing you. I just wanted to pick up one or two of the tools we left here yesterday. My mother lost a couple of roof tiles in the storm and I'm fixing them for her.' He nods at the shutters. 'You're doing a good job there,' he says chivalrously, choosing to ignore the fact that I've clearly bodged things terribly on my first attempt.

'However,' he continues solicitously, 'if you would allow me to make a suggestion, you might find it easier to take the shutters down before you sand them. You'll probably find it a bit more stable on solid ground,' he can't resist adding with a cheeky grin.

I attempt to regain my composure, concentrating on the shutters with what I hope appears to be an air of competent efficiency. 'Why, yes, of course. They're just a little heavy for me to take down on my own.'

And in fact it hadn't even occurred to me that this might be a possibility, but on closer inspection it looks like they'll simply lift off their hinges quite easily.

In the space of a couple of minutes, Cédric has taken the shutters off all the windows and piled them in a neat stack on the grass. 'I believe your aunt had a pair of trestles in the shed,' he says, leading the way.

So that's what those wooden frames are – I did wonder.

'You'll be wanting to put a good primer on them after you've finished the sanding. Mr. Bricolage has ones for exterior woodwork. Look for one marked for extreme conditions. The weather here can be pretty wild, as you've already discovered.'

Ah, so that's where I went wrong. Primer.

'Yes, of course. I was intending getting just that,' I say.

'The large shutters on the doors are very heavy,' he continues. 'But you have enough to be getting on with here, and then tomorrow, when my brothers and I return, we'll lift the others off for you.'

As he finishes speaking, there's the sound of car tyres coming up the drive and we both turn to see who it is. *Great*, I think. *Someone else dropping by, just to ensure my humiliation is complete.*

My heart sinks still further as Nigel Yates pulls up beside us and jumps out. He comes round the side of the car and embraces me like a long-lost friend. 'My dear Gina,' he exclaims, ignoring Cédric. 'I heard you'd had some damage in that awful storm the other night. Thought I'd come to the rescue!'

Heard how? I wonder fleetingly, the power of the bush telegraph in a small rural community still a novelty to me.

'Cédric Thibault, Nigel Yates.' I make the introductions so he has to turn to acknowledge Cédric, who is standing by patiently with a polite smile on his face.

'Monsieur,' Nigel says with a curt nod.

'Cédric and his brothers are stonemasons. They very kindly came yesterday to patch up the worst of the damage and are coming back tomorrow to carry on with the job. So it's good of you to come by, but thanks to the Thibaults, everything's under control.'

Instead of sharing my delight at this fortunate turn of events, Nigel appears somewhat annoyed. He spots the pile of shutters. 'And are they fixing shutters for you as well?' he asks.

'*Non*,' replies Cédric, who has clearly understood the gist of our conversation. 'Mademoiselle Gina is undertaking that work herself.

I was just giving her a hand taking the shutters down. In fact, now that you're here, perhaps we can remove the larger ones too.'

'Of course,' replies Nigel in a tone that suggests he is man enough for any such challenge, and he removes his jacket, arranging it somewhat fussily across the back seat of his car. I can't help but compare the slight flabbiness of his stomach beneath his neatly tucked-in shirt with the firm muscularity of Cédric's midriff under his clean white T-shirt.

Leading the way, Nigel seizes the first large shutter beside the front door and heaves it upwards, but it doesn't budge. Cédric produces a hammer and chisel and, with a few deft taps, loosens the hinges. Taking a side each, the men lift the heavy wooden panel and carry it over to lean it against a tree beside the trestles. Cédric balances the weight with the easy grace of a man accustomed to physical labour. They repeat the exercise until all the door shutters have been removed, by which time Nigel's face is looking distinctly red and shiny and the long, carefully arranged strands of hair covering his receding hairline have flopped free and are hanging down, in a somewhat alarming style, over one ear. Damp stains have appeared under the sleeves of his shirt, the tail of which has come adrift from his waistband.

Though, of course, I'm hardly in a position to criticise, given my own scruffy state.

Cédric, on the other hand, remains neatly unruffled and hardly seems to have exerted himself at all.

When they've finished, there's an awkward pause. 'Would anyone like a glass of water?' I ask, to fill it.

Nigel accepts with alacrity, combing his hair with his fingers to plaster the wayward locks back into position.

'*Non merci*,' says Cédric. 'I must get on with fixing my mother's roof.' He picks up a box of tools. 'See you tomorrow, Gina,' he says, shaking my hand, 'and *bonne continuation* with your work.' He nods and politely proffers a hand to Nigel. 'Monsieur.'

Once Cédric disappears down the drive, Nigel turns to me. 'You want to be careful about who you use to do work on your house, you know, Gina. You can't just ask the first cowboy who comes along. And French workmen can be tricky. I've got an excellent English builder whom I use. I'll phone him for you first thing tomorrow and ask him to come by and look at what needs doing.'

'Thank you, but that won't be necessary,' I say firmly, trying not to let my annoyance show. 'The Thibault brothers are extremely experienced and I'm lucky to have them.'

'But surely it's difficult communicating – how will you tell them what you want done?'

'That won't be a problem,' I reply shortly. 'I speak excellent French.'

As long as you ignore the occasional complete foot-in-mouth bloomer, I think. And also the fact that I haven't the first clue about roof construction in English, never mind in French, so I have no idea what I want done. Other than the fact that I want it all put back to how it was, and preferably so that it won't blow down again in the next storm either.

Nigel is clearly not picking up, from the warning note in my voice, the fact that he's seriously beginning to annoy me. 'Well, I just hope they're not ripping you off,' he persists. 'What's their quote for the job? They tend to have one price for the French and one for the English, you know.'

I don't want to admit to him that I haven't had a quote, that in fact I haven't asked at all what this is going to cost. 'They're giving me an excellent price and I'm more than satisfied that they'll do a good job. They come very highly recommended.'

By their own mother, admittedly.

'So thank you for your offer of help, but I've got it all under control,' I end firmly. 'Now, if you've finished your water, please excuse me. I must get back to my sanding.'

I hold out a hand to take the glass from him.

'Well, I'll be interested to see how you get on. Let me know if you have any problems with the work. I just hope they get it finished before they bugger off on holiday for most of August. The French do, you know. Remember, I'm always here if you need anything. Us expats have to stick together!' And with a slightly damp peck on each cheek, he finally departs.

'Yuk,' I say, rubbing my face and watching his car disappear. And with renewed energy, I plug myself back in to my phone, turning the volume up high again, and take out my irritation at Nigel and my frustration at the unattainability of Mr Blue Pickup on the next shutter.

Chapter 9

By the end of the following week, my life is feeling a little more under control. Oh, I'm still upset and angry, to the point of nausea, whenever I allow myself to think about that photo of Dad and to speculate about Liz's affair with him – no wonder she said meeting the love of her life had been an impossible situation! But I've pretty much managed to shrug off the frustration and disappointment of discovering that Cédric is safely married with two children. I try not to let myself think about any of it much, immersing myself in sandpaper and sage-green paint: denial and distraction seem to be by far the best strategies for coping at the moment.

Tonight I've got the welcome distraction of company for once. We may not have much in common, but Hugh and Celia are coming for an evening drink and I find I'm very much looking forward to seeing them. I used to think they were a bit stuffy, but now feel ashamed of my ingratitude: they've been nothing but kind and helpful since I took up residence at Liz's. We sit on the terrace with a bottle of *blanc sec* on the table before us, condensation forming a thirst-quenching dew on the glasses before us, even before we take the first sip.

Celia raises her glass. 'Cheers, Gina. You've had quite a fortnight, but you seem to have coped admirably and I'm sure it can only get better.'

I lift my glass in return and take the first sip of my cool wine, savouring the balance and depth of the flavour.

If only you knew, I think. The roof has been an almost welcome diversion from the discovery about my father. For all I know, the affair may have continued until he died. I wonder how I can bring the conversation round nonchalantly to the subject of Dad, to see whether the Everetts know anything about the timing and frequency of his possible visits here.

But Hugh's more interested in the progress of my roof than in idle chit-chat. He tips his head back to look up at the scaffolding that still encases the wall of the house.

'You know, Gina, you were terribly lucky getting the Thibault brothers, and at such short notice. They're the best in the area, real craftsmen. Everyone wants them for their building projects. There's usually a six-month wait. You've obviously charmed them.'

'Hmm, I think it was more the fact that their mother ordered them to do it than anything to do with me. I'm very lucky to have a neighbour who wields so much clout,' I say, hoping my brisk tone will make up for the fact that my face has flushed scarlet at the thought of one of the brothers in particular.

'Poor you, though,' chips in Celia. 'All that added expense – and on something as boring as a roof.'

'Yes, boring but rather essential, as I rapidly realised once I didn't actually have one any more. But I've been incredibly lucky there, too. The insurance assessor came straight round when I called him after the storm and they're going to cover quite a bit of the cost. The Thibaults have given me a very reasonable price for the rest of the job, so thankfully it's not going to make too much of a dent in my redundancy money.'

Hugh looks at the roof appraisingly. 'Looks like they've replaced the tiles over a very large area, though. That's quite a significant amount of work. Their mother's clout obviously extends to the brothers' billing philosophy too. You really do have friends in high places, if you'll forgive the pun,' he smiles, with a nod at the scaffolding.

'Well, all's well that ends well,' says Celia. 'Looks like you've been busy yourself, too. The shutters are looking very elegant. Bravo!' Celia congratulates me. 'Now then,' she continues, 'it's time you took a break from all this and had a bit of a social life instead. Next Tuesday's the fourteenth, you know. Bastille Day. We're taking a big table at the festivities in Gensac and we'd love it if you could come along. It's great fun. They put up long trestle tables in the *place* and there's a meal. Everyone brings their own plates and cutlery and you can buy bottles of wine from local producers. Afterwards there are fireworks and dancing. Do come – it's quite the social event of the year.'

It does sound fun and suddenly I realise that it would be nice to have a break from my own company and an evening out.

'That would be lovely.'

'Come to us first. You can leave the car and we'll walk into the village together,' Celia beams.

'Delighted you can join us,' says Hugh. 'I hope you'll save the first dance for me.' He raises his glass for another sip. 'Now, tell us all about this Master of Wine course you're going to be doing . . .'

A while later, as they get up to go, Hugh turns to me as if something's just occurred to him and says casually – a shade too casually perhaps, 'By the way, Gina, a few days ago the funeral parlour asked me what we are intending to do with Liz's ashes. The law is very strict in France – you can't just scatter them where you want. I know it's a bit soon, and maybe you haven't decided yet, but I told them we're taking them back to England, just to buy you a bit more time. That's one point Liz didn't cover in her will. I persuaded them to let me collect the urn and we have it safely back at our house. We'll be happy to hang on to them for as long as you like. No rush. Just thought you should know that they're there whenever you decide you want them.'

I'm a bit taken aback. I'd completely forgotten about them. And what on earth do I want to do with them now?

'Okay. Thanks, Hugh,' I say briskly. 'I'll have a think and let you know.'

So that's another sleepless night as I toss and turn in the bed in the spare room, to where I decamped after the storm, wondering what the right thing would be to do with the final bodily remains of my favourite aunt. My mother's sister. My friend.

My father's lover.

◆ ◆ ◆

I'm up early the next morning and head down to Sainte-Foy for the Saturday market. Liz always used to say, 'You have to get there before all the English appear if you want the best produce. Fortunately, though, they only manage to get themselves out of bed by about eleven o'clock so it's just the last hour that's a complete scrum.'

I love browsing at the hundreds of stalls that line the narrow streets of the old *bastide* town. There's certainly variety, with everything from cheap clothes and tacky knock-off jewellery to delicious local produce and pretty arts and crafts. I'm standing in the queue at my favourite fruit stall, waiting to buy some of the mouth-wateringly juicy yellow nectarines that have just come into season, when I feel a small tug at my sleeve.

I turn to find Nathalie in the queue behind me.

'*Bonjour*, Mam'selle Gina,' she says, and I bend to plant the customary two kisses on her upturned face.

The attractive woman beside her extends a hand in greeting. '*Bonjour*, Mademoiselle Peplow. I am Marie-Louise Thibault. I've heard a lot about you. Pleased to meet you. I hope the work on your roof hasn't been too disruptive for you?'

So this must be Cédric's wife. She has a cloud of dark curly hair, cheekbones like Audrey Hepburn's, and is wearing slim jeans and a crisp white shirt. She looks effortlessly and understatedly sexy in the way that only certain Frenchwomen can.

Her hand is soft and immaculately manicured, and I am uncomfortably conscious of my own cracked palms and tattered, broken nails, roughened from working on the shutters day in, day out, as I take it in mine. Her handshake is firmly friendly.

I assure Marie-Louise that the work is progressing well. 'I'm very grateful to your husband and his brothers for getting it done so quickly.'

'Yes, it's lucky. I think they said they should just be able to get it finished before we go on holiday. We're off to the *bassin* at Arcachon in a week's time, you know, aren't we, Nathalie?'

I didn't know. I feel a pang of disappointment that the job will be finished so soon. I've enjoyed having the brothers around this week, their banter and laughter in the background a friendly accompaniment to my painting duties on the other side of the house.

And I shall miss the afternoon tea breaks, which have become a daily occurrence, with Pierre and Cédric. Most of all Cédric. Not that we have time for deep and meaningful discussions but, as we perch companionably on the terrace wall cradling our mugs of tea, I'm always acutely conscious of the current of attraction that ebbs and flows between us. It's become the highlight of my lonely days, I realise. And then quickly dismiss the thought, before Marie-Louise can read my guilty mind.

'*Oui*, I'm really looking forward to swimming,' Nathalie chimes in. 'But even more I'm looking forward to Thursday evening. It's

Bastille Day, you know, Mam'selle Gina. We're going to buy me a new dress after we've finished shopping here.'

Marie-Louise smooths the little girl's fine, dark hair, a gesture that is so full of love it makes my throat ache. 'We are indeed. Because you've grown so much in the last few months and nothing fits.' She smiles at me.

'Well, I'll be there too, so I'll look forward to seeing you,' I say.

'Good,' says Nathalie. 'It's such fun.' Then she looks momentarily worried. 'But you must shut Lafite inside. He won't like it if he hears the fireworks, you know. They'll scare him.'

'Don't worry,' I reassure her. 'I'll leave him some extra food and put on some soothing music that he likes, so he won't hear the bangs.'

'Good idea,' nods the little girl solemnly.

Marie-Louise touches my arm lightly. The gold of the wedding ring on her left hand winks cheerfully – mockingly, it seems to me – in the sunshine. 'It's your turn now, Mademoiselle.' She nods towards the stallholder.

My nectarines safely stashed in my basket, I turn to say goodbye, but Marie-Louise is already engaged in conversation with the lady behind the stall. Nathalie gives me a little wave, and I feel a pang of protective love for the child that takes me by surprise.

Until now, the sum total of my experience with children has been the occasional lunch party at the houses of married friends, where swarms of Baby Gap-clad mini-mes clamour for attention and the proceedings deteriorate inevitably into noisy, sticky or even (horror of horrors!) smelly chaos. But Nathalie, with her serious, trusting eyes and earnest little face, which brightens up like the sun coming out from behind a cloud when she smiles, has a way of tugging at my heartstrings. I wish I had a daughter like her, so that I could hold her hand and make her laugh and hug her until the clouds were banished for good.

I raise my hand in a little wave, resisting the urge to smooth her hair as Marie-Louise has just done. 'See you on Thursday,' I say, and allow myself to be swept up by the strengthening current of the market throng. So that I don't have to dwell on the fact that this encounter has reminded me I am still very much an outsider here. And at this precise moment I would sell my soul for a husband like Cédric and a daughter like Nathalie, so I'd never feel such overwhelming loneliness again.

◆ ◆ ◆

I'm standing in front of the wardrobe in the spare room, dispassionately regarding my reflection in the soft, freckled silver of the mirror, which is misty with age around the edges. Despite copious slatherings of sunscreen, my skin has turned a rich golden brown from hours spent sanding and painting in the hot July sun. My hair, usually a rather boring mouse colour, now has expensive-looking highlights of streaky blonde, also courtesy of the sun's bleaching rays. I've had a long lukewarm bath, soaking and scrubbing away the dust and paint spots, and have treated my thirsty skin to the last precious drops of my body lotion. And I've put on and taken off at least a dozen different outfits, which are now deposited in muddled heaps on the bed.

Bastille Night and I haven't got a thing to wear.

With a sigh, I pick up a black summer dress and pull it over my head for the second time in ten minutes. It's not right – much too formal – and, besides, the only shoes that go with it are a pair of high-heeled sandals that guarantee a sprained ankle, at the very least, when walking over the stones of Gensac's pretty *place*. I peel off the dress again and wrench open the wardrobe door. The Ossie Clark tunic gleams seductively on its hanger. I've purposely been avoiding it, even though it's the one thing I really want to wear and

I know it would be perfect for this evening. But it would feel like a betrayal now to wear anything of Liz's.

Maybe she even wore it when she was with my father. I push the thought out of my head.

I rifle through the other clothes left in the wardrobe, in the vain hope that something else will leap out at me as being the perfect solution to my sartorial dilemma. But any possibilities have already been taken out, tried on and discarded on the bed. Methodically, I return each of them to their hangers and put them back where they belong. I glance at my watch, which tells me time has now run out. And then quickly, so I won't think about it any more, I pull on a pair of flowing linen trousers, wrench the vintage top from the rail and slip it over my head. As the cool silk drapes itself against my tanned skin, I know that, conscience or no conscience, this is what I'm wearing.

Anyway, she probably never did wear it with Dad. And if she did, that has nothing to do with here and now, I tell my reflection in the mirror.

I buckle on a pair of strappy sandals and give my hair a final comb before going through to the kitchen. We're far enough away from both Gensac and Sainte-Foy that I doubt the noise of the fireworks will be anything more than a series of very muffled pops at the most, but a sudden vision of Nathalie's serious little face makes me pour extra food into Lafite's bowl and turn on some soothing music. Attracted by the sound of the food pattering into his bowl, rather than Kiri Te Kanawa's singing, I suspect, the old cat appears and rubs himself fondly against my ankle. 'Now, you're staying in tonight and I, for once, am going out,' I tell him, gently stroking his furry cheek. I leave him happily munching, pick up a basket containing my plate, cutlery and glass for the meal, and lock the door behind me.

The narrow streets of Gensac are abuzz with people hurrying towards the open square in the middle of the village, all carrying cheerily clinking bags and baskets. Strings of red, white and blue bunting overhead mark the way, and above them swifts dart and soar in the opal sky as if sharing the excitement of the chattering crowd below. Hugh, Celia and I join the gathering throng and, turning the corner, pause to take in the scene in the *place* before us.

The square has been transformed from its daytime serenity into a humming party venue. Long trestle tables are arranged before us, and groups of people are gathering round each one, chattering and embracing as they greet one another and then set out their glasses and cutlery on the white paper table covers. Under the soaring plane tree that dominates the heart of the village, a wooden dance floor has been laid out and the mayor begins testing the public address system through a microphone, somewhat reluctantly handed over by the DJ from behind the flashing façade of his disco. Red and white streamers radiate from the tree to form a fluttering canopy above our heads, and golden fairy lights are just starting to gleam as the dusk deepens. And in and out of everything, small children dart and race, unwittingly mirroring the flight of the swifts high above us all.

We hand over a few euros in exchange for strips of tickets that entitle us to each of the four courses of tonight's meal. Celia cranes her neck and then waves. 'There are the others. I told them to bag a table if they got here before us.'

We pick our way between the trestles to join the rest of our party, who are already well established by the look of the open bottles of wine arranged the length of the table. Celia pretends not to notice as Nigel, looking as rosily damp as ever, waves me over, gesticulating at the empty space on the bench beside him. 'Gina, I've saved you a seat!' He clambers to his feet and embraces me somewhat stickily. There's nothing for it but to sit down next to him, but I'm relieved to notice that the Everetts take up their places across from us and Hugh gives me a reassuring wink as he settles himself at the table.

'Let me pour you some wine,' says Nigel, enthusiastically sloshing some of the local co-op's finest (which isn't at all bad, actually) into my glass.

'Just a half, thanks – I'm driving,' I say, firmly putting my hand over the top. I've taken the precaution of including a large bottle of water in my basket and I place this on the table between us, signalling my clear intention not to succumb to any further temptations he may try to put my way.

Hugh introduces me to the large lady sitting on the other side of me and, to my relief, she engages me in an animated conversation about the forthcoming Franco-British week in Sainte-Foy, which apparently includes a French versus English *boules* tournament in which she is very keen that I should participate.

Above the crowd's noisy crescendo, the loudspeakers on either side of the disco give a sudden shriek of feedback, and the mayor declares the proceedings officially open with a hearty welcome, inviting us to take our plates and make our way to the serving tables at the top of the *place* where we will be given our starters.

Despite the hordes of people, the queues move surprisingly quickly, the servers obviously long practised in their efficiency in doling out slices of charcuterie and hunks of crusty bread on to each outstretched plate in turn. And besides, the queues are a further opportunity to mingle, greet more friends and exchange gossip as the tide of partygoers swirls and eddies between the tables.

'So how's your roof coming on?' asks Nigel, returning to his seat close on my heels and tucking into the array of garlic-spiked pâté and cold meats on the plate before him.

'Very well indeed, thank you,' I retort, trying to keep the edge of irritation and defensiveness out of my voice. 'The Thibaults are doing an excellent job. They'll have the outside pretty much done by the end of the week. Then they're off on holiday for a fortnight. They'll be back to finish off and replaster the ceiling in August but there's no great hurry for that.'

'Typical French workmen,' he sniffs. 'It's impossible to get anything done at all in the summer. You'll be lucky if you see them again before September. I'm surprised they're doing the plastering. Surely you need a proper plasterer for that? Mind you, they're impossible to come by. Expensive work, too. Let me know if you want one who speaks English. I can ask my builder for you if you like.'

'Thank you, but I have every confidence in the Thibaults and I'm sure they'll be back to finish the job. Their mother is a neighbour of mine and she'll chase them up for me if need be.' I've got a sneaking suspicion that they're doing the plastering themselves as a favour to keep costs down for me, but I'm not going to share this thought with Nigel.

I take a sip of the rough red wine, pausing to enjoy the way the robustly tannic local brew complements the fattiness of the spicy charcuterie.

Across the square at another of the long tables, I spot Mireille and her family. All four sons are there and I see Luc and Nathalie sitting between Cédric and Marie-Louise, happily tucking into their meal, surrounded by assorted aunts and cousins. Their diminutive grandmother holds court at one end of the long wooden bench, pausing frequently over her starter to greet a constant stream of friends and neighbours who come up to talk to her.

Celia leans across the table, following my gaze. 'Isn't that Madame Thibault?' she asks. 'We must go and say hello later on. And that tall lady on the next table along is our local novelist, Abigail Peters. Have you read any of her books? Quite a celebrity in these parts.' She pauses to scan the square for other noteworthy

93

characters. 'You see the woman on the next table but one? The one that looks a bit like Carla Bruni? Well, she's a ballet dancer from Paris. She and her husband have bought a wreck of a château and are doing it up. That's him at this end of the table – rather dishy.'

She breaks off to half rise and greet Monsieur le Maire, who is doing the rounds of the tables, encouraging people to make their way back to the serving tables with their empty plates to collect the main course. He shakes my hand and pronounces himself to be '*Enchanté*' to make my acquaintance.

'Shall we . . . ?' says Nigel, picking up his plate and sliding off the bench to allow me to go first. We file up to join the queues once again. As I stand in the line, I feel a gentle tug on my sleeve and turn round to find Cédric and Nathalie behind me, also with their plates in their hands. My heart does a triple somersault.

'*Bonsoir*, Mam'selle Gina,' says Nathalie, who is still holding on to the silky sleeve of my tunic. I bend to kiss her on each cheek. 'I like your outfit,' she says shyly. 'Papa, doesn't she look elegant?'

'She does indeed,' smiles Cédric gallantly. And then, to my surprise, he also leans in to kiss me twice and I feel myself blushing involuntarily where his slightly rough cheek has brushed mine. A jolt of attraction, like static electricity, crackles in the air between us.

To cover my confusion, I bend back towards Nathalie. 'And you look absolutely beautiful,' I say. 'Is that your new dress? It's so pretty.'

The little girl beams. '*Oui*. Yellow is my favourite colour,' she replies. 'And how is Lafite? Did you shut him in safely?'

'Yes, I left him listening to a little Mozart so I think he'll be fine.'

Nigel, who's been chatting to some of the other members of our party, turns towards me and, to my intense annoyance, puts a proprietorial – and somewhat clammy – hand on the small of my back to usher me forward. 'Here you go, Gina, it's our turn next.'

I smile again at Nathalie and Cédric. 'Would you like to go first?' I offer.

'That's very kind, but we'll wait for the rest of the family,' says Cédric, and I see that Luc, Marie-Louise and the others are getting up from their table. '*Bonsoir*, Monsieur,' he adds politely to Nigel, who gives him a rather curt nod in reply.

'Okay. Well, *bonne continuation*,' I say, telling myself that the sense of disappointment that washes over me is completely out of line and must be ignored.

As I make my way back to the table, my plate piled high with chicken and rice, I make a small detour to say hello to Mireille, who has now joined the queue with the rest of her family. I kiss her, Marie-Louise and Luc and greet the brothers, including Pierre, who juggles mobile phone and plate to shake my hand. But then I move on swiftly so I won't hold them up in getting their meal. They are in the middle of a noisy, merry throng of friends and I'm an outsider here. And, besides, my food's getting cold, I tell myself, to divert the tide of self-pity that's threatening to overwhelm me.

The cheerful cacophony of clinking glasses, clattering cutlery and chattering voices grows louder than ever as the meal nears its end, cheeses and choc ices following the main course. Finally, the mayor and his band of helpers circulate with bin bags to collect the debris and plates are scraped thoroughly before being stowed carefully back into bags and baskets, the decks cleared for the evening's main events. Darkness has now fallen and the fairy lights sparkle merrily beneath their canopy of paper streamers, replicated above, several millionfold, by the Milky Way. The DJ takes his place behind the bank of flashing lights and suddenly music floods the square and there's a tidal surge towards the dance floor as couples begin to spin and sway to a Johnny Hallyday number. Small boys, fuelled up on ice cream and excitement now, race in and out of the dancers, while groups of little girls, in pretty dresses with their hair tied up in jaunty red, white and blue bows, hop solemnly and a little self-consciously on the edge of the bobbing, spinning throng.

I'm chatting to Hugh and some of the others sitting around the table, whose white paper cover is now festively printed with silver grease spots and pink circles of wine, when suddenly I'm aware that Nigel is trying hard to attract my attention. He's drunk most of his bottle of wine and it hasn't done much to enhance his charms. His face is flushed a deep shade of magenta, clashing violently with his pink shirt, and his features, framed by their strands of sweat-slicked hair, have slackened and sagged. I studiously try to ignore this beguiling apparition bobbing increasingly persistently on the periphery of my vision. But then he puts a sticky hand on my upper arm, leaving a damp paw-print on the silk of my sleeve.

Hugh, seeing my plight, leaps to his feet with alacrity and reaches a hand across the table. 'Now, Gina, I believe we have a date for the first dance,' he says. 'Nigel, if you'll excuse us?'

He leads me to the dance floor.

'Thank you. That was kind,' I say.

'Probably just a stay of execution, I'm afraid,' he grins. 'Don't think you're going to get away without a dance with him. But we can at least show him how it's done.'

To my surprise, Hugh commences an accomplished jive, leading me so that I quickly pick up the steps and am soon happily hopping and twirling. 'This is fun!' I shriek, as he whisks me round the dance floor. 'Where did you learn to dance like this?'

'On our five-year posting to Senegal there wasn't much else to do. The expats, mostly French, ran ceroc classes, and Celia and I signed up. We even won the dance-off at the Christmas party one year. First prize: a bottle of the local hooch. Second prize: two bottles of the local hooch.'

He steers me deftly round another bobbing couple.

'Shame your mother isn't here for the party. Will she be coming to visit you soon?'

'No plans,' I shout above the beat of the music, as our orbit has now brought us alongside one of the banks of speakers that flank the disco's flashing lights.

'It's a pity she couldn't come more often when your father was over on his tasting trips, but I suppose she was quite tied up at home then, with you at school and so on.'

I miss a turn and stumble clumsily.

'Whoops – I've got you,' he laughs.

'So, did Dad come here often?' I ask, hoping the question sounds casual despite the fact that I'm shouting to make myself heard above the music.

'Not here so much, no. We only saw David in this neck of the woods once or twice. Mostly he was being wined and dined by the great and the good in Bordeaux. A tough assignment! But it was his work, after all, so maybe Catherine felt she didn't want to be in the way. A pity, though. Liz would have enjoyed her company.'

Yes, I think, unless Liz was too busy enjoying Dad's company instead.

I want to ask him more, but the music slows as the song comes to an end and Hugh makes a mock bow and kisses my hand. 'Thank you, my dear. That was most enjoyable and you are an excellent partner.'

We pick our way back to the table where, I'm relieved to find, Celia has engaged Nigel in an animated conversation about the best local sources of click-lock flooring, a subject on which he apparently holds strong and expert opinions. I settle down to watch the swirl of the dancers as the music starts up again. It seems the whole of the local community is here and the full cross-section of ages, shapes and sizes is on display.

I feel a tap on my shoulder and turn to find Cédric standing there, a bottle of wine in one hand and two empty glasses in the other.

And maybe it's the heat or the wine or the music, but all of a sudden it's as if the crowd fades away, leaving just the two of us in a space quite apart from everything and everyone else. I stand, feeling myself drawn to him without a word being spoken. Someone pushes past behind me and I'm forced in closer, suddenly dizzy with longing as my arm brushes against Cédric's. I feel a jolt of heat, which has nothing to do with the warmth of the evening air and the crush of bodies around us, and everything to do with the fact that our eyes lock, in a gaze of such intense mutual desire that I think I may just melt into his arms here and now. For a long moment we hold one another with this look, naked in our unspoken hunger. It's completely unambiguous. There's no way I can explain it away. And surely everyone around us must be able to see it too, to sense the heat that flows between us. The language of desire needs no translation.

I pull myself up short in the sudden realisation that 'everyone' includes his wife, mother and children, not to mention assorted brothers, cousins, uncles and aunts, and pretty much anyone he's ever known. The spell is broken and he drops his gaze, downcast, as I draw away from him again, even though it takes every last shred of my willpower to make myself do it.

I try to ignore the disappointment and hurt that are written clearly in his eyes, behind the warmth of his undeniably sexy smile.

He gestures with the wine bottle and glasses. 'I wondered if you'd like to try this. It's a local wine, made by friends of mine. They've just won a medal for it.' He pours a little of the velvety red liquid into each of the glasses and offers me one. To cover up the fact that my hands are shaking, in time with the trembling of my knees, I raise it to my lips and sip. My eyes widen in surprise.

If it weren't for the fact that I know it's local, I'd have guessed this was from the Médoc. It has the complexity and subtlety of its smarter and more expensive neighbours. Cédric grins, delighted at my response.

'Your friends certainly know what they're doing. What's the name of the château?' He turns the bottle so that I can see the label, which reads 'Château de la Chapelle' and bears the logo of the Sainte-Foy Bordeaux *appellation*. I lean in closer to get a better look, and as I do, I sense again the heat of his body, and my head spins. He's watching me intently, his dark eyes serious for a moment, and I get the impression he's about to say something more.

But the moment is shattered when suddenly we're rudely interrupted. Nigel has materialised at my side, flushed with the excitement of yet another opportunity to demonstrate his extensive knowledge of the local DIY trade, or perhaps it's just the effect of one more glass of wine.

'There you are, Gina,' he slurs, putting an overly familiar arm round my shoulders. 'That was quite a display you and old Hugh put on, on the dance floor. Care to put me through my paces next?'

'That would have been lovely,' I say, smiling politely while firmly removing his arm, 'but the music seems to have stopped.' I turn back to Cédric, but he has gone. I catch a glimpse of him as he picks his way back through the throng to his family, and my throat constricts with disappointment.

The mayor has retaken the microphone and is announcing that the firework display is about to begin, if everyone would like to make their way to the viewing point.

Chattering and laughing, the crowd flows through the gap at the end of the square and regroups where the hillside falls away steeply to the darkened valley floor below. I try to manoeuvre so that several other members of our party are between me and Nigel, but he's sticking to me like glue ('sticking' being the operative word), persistently edging rather too far into my personal space. I catch sight of the Thibaults over to our right. Pierre has lifted Nathalie on to his shoulders so she can see and she's giggling and holding on tight to his dark curls. Cédric, standing next to them, catches my eye and raises a hand in faint salute, but he's unsmiling now, his face expressionless. Luc has joined a gang of young boys who are buzzing with excitement at the front of the crowd. They are repeatedly shooed back by the mayor, although it's like trying to herd a swarm of flies.

The first rocket explodes above us and all faces turn to the starlit sky. All except one, that is. Out of the corner of my eye, in the flashes of coloured light that illuminate the scene, I'm acutely aware that Cédric is watching me, rather than the fireworks.

The only sounds for the next quarter of an hour are the cracks of gunpowder and the oohs and aahs of delight. They've put on quite a show in this village, and the same thing is happening all across France as, for one night at least, her people unite to celebrate the *liberté, egalité* and *fraternité* of their Republic.

When the display is over, the music starts up again in the square, enticing the partygoers back to the disco. Some people begin to drift homewards and I head back to our table, intending to retrieve my basket and make my way back to the car parked in the Everetts' drive. But I'm intercepted by Nigel, who grabs my hand and pulls me on to the dance floor.

One of my favourite songs of the summer begins to play; I've heard it often on the radio. It's a pulsing tune that has everyone up on their feet. Its words are a poignant invitation to all who are alone to come and join the dance and they seem to be directed at people like Liz used to be, or like my mother is now, making their way on their own through life. People like me.

Or, indeed, like Nigel, who is now gyrating energetically in front of me. He appears to have no inhibitions on the dance floor, although sadly he also appears to have no sense of rhythm. All around us, couples have taken to the floor and all ages, shapes and sizes whirl by in formation. Little old ladies dressed in black dance past in decorous pairs. Hugh and Celia ceroc on by in perfect harmony. The Carla Bruni ballet dancer and her dishy husband whirl past elegantly. And the tall lady novelist waltzes by, clutching Monsieur le Maire to her ample bosom. And in the middle of it all, Nigel and I hop clumsily, out of sync with the music and with each other. What he lacks in style he makes up for in enthusiasm, though, and I duck to avoid his flailing arms, at the end of which his fingers are clicking, a move that's straight out of the Austin Powers School of Groovy Dancing.

He moves in closer, so I step back to try to maintain a bit of distance between us, and in doing so tread heavily on the foot of the dancer behind me, who staggers and bumps into his own part-ner, almost sending her flying. And my mortification is complete as I realise the couple are Cédric and Marie-Louise. I shout an apology, but he has caught her and they whirl off, orbiting in their own accomplished jive, he with a smile and a shake of his head and she laughing as she spins away and back again into the steadying embrace of his outstretched arm.

The music finishes and, before it can segue into the next song, I thank Nigel and firmly turn and walk off the dance floor. He trots happily behind me, obviously pleased with his performance. We reach the table and he ensures my chagrin is complete with what is – as far as I'm concerned – his parting shot. 'You know, Gina, you're really not that bad a dancer.'

◆ ◆ ◆

Hugh, Celia and I walk back through the quiet streets of the village, the music and lights in the square fading behind us, and pick our way carefully the hundred yards or so along the darkened country road to the driveway of their house. They've left lights on, which shine welcoming golden squares on to the gravel in front of the house.

'Come in and have a cup of coffee,' the Everetts urge.

I hesitate. I wouldn't normally, but there is something I want to do, so I accept. While Celia bustles around boiling the kettle and clinking cups and saucers in the kitchen, Hugh opens the French doors and we settle ourselves on their terrace, the night air still warm, the noise of cicadas drowning out the distant sounds of the continuing revelry in the *place*.

Nonchalantly, as if it's a thought that's just occurred to me and not something I've mulled over endlessly through the dark hours of several recent sleepless nights, I say, 'By the way, Hugh, since I'm here I might as well take away Liz's urn. If it's not inconvenient for you, of course.'

'Why, yes, not at all,' he replies, glancing at me astutely. 'We'll get it on your way out. Have you decided what you're going to do with it?'

Neither of us can quite bring ourselves to mention the word 'ashes'.

'Not yet, but I think she should be back in her own home until I do decide.'

Celia appears with a tray of elegant china and the conversation turns to a review of the evening's festivities, and some final snippets of gossip about the other members of our party (it turns out the husband of the large woman sitting next to me ran off with their cleaning lady a year ago – 'They've moved to Gardonne and he's gone almost native! Poor Vanessa – so brave of her to stay on, though of course Franco-British week keeps her busy.').

As I take my leave, Hugh dives into his study and reappears with a cardboard box, which he stows carefully on the floor of my car by the passenger seat. 'Mind how you go, Gina,' he says in his gruff-yet-kind manner. I hug them both goodbye.

It's well after 1 a.m. when I get home, and Lafite runs out with an affronted squawk when I push open the door, indignant at having been incarcerated for the evening.

I set the cardboard box down on the kitchen table and open the flaps. Inside there's a neat black casket. I close the box again, disguising the obscenity of death behind the plain brown packaging. It's too late to decide where to put it tonight. I'll think about it in the morning.

◆ ◆ ◆

And so, of course, at 2 a.m. I'm wide awake and staring at the spare-room ceiling. Lafite is curled up in a neat ball at the end of the bed, sleeping peacefully. But my mind is racing. That cup of coffee at the Everetts' was definitely a mistake.

I can't stop replaying that moment when I thought Cédric was going to say something more. What would it have been? Something along the lines of 'Fancy an affair?', I suppose. Just like every other cheating scumbag, I think bitterly.

But he seems so different, not at all the type, says the voice of hope. Don't be naive, it's the French national pastime, says the voice of realism.

To distract myself from this frustrating cycle of thoughts – which is getting me nowhere, least of all to sleep – I turn my mind to the cardboard box on the kitchen table. Where am I going to scatter Liz's ashes and where am I going to store the casket until I get around to the act of scattering? Rationally, of course, it's just a pile of dust. Earth to earth and all that. But you can't get away from the fact that this dust is the last remnant of Liz's physical presence. And something that's been so dear and so familiar deserves – demands – to be treated with respect. No, respect is too cold a word. With love. Whatever she might have been to my father, she was a wonderful aunt – and friend – to me. One of the people on this planet who really loved me. And there aren't very many of those left, I reflect with a sudden rush of self-pity.

Sorry, but four o'clock in the morning really is the loneliest of hours.

I pull myself together. Okay, forget about where to scatter her ashes for the moment. Let's just decide where to put the damn urn in the meantime.

I don't think I can bring myself to put it on the mantelpiece in the kitchen. It would put me off my food to sit looking at a jar of mortal remains every mealtime. I could keep it in the study, but I'll be spending quite a bit of time in there when I really get started on my coursework and I don't want it to be a constant distraction. I could stick it in the broom cupboard in the utility room and try to forget about it, but that seems far too callous, so it'd be on my conscience. Which would mean I couldn't forget about it at all.

The sitting room seems like the best compromise. It's not a room Liz ever really used much, but it seems respectful, with the air of formality that death demands, and at the same time is slightly out of the way of my daily life.

I know I'm not going to be able to get to sleep until I've moved the urn, so I slide out of bed carefully so as not to disturb Lafite and pad through to the kitchen. The house is so quiet, all I can hear is the soft heartbeat tick of the clock above the fireplace. I fill the kettle and switch it on, pretending that a cup of camomile tea is just the soothing antidote I need to get back to sleep, but really to ruffle the surface of the silence with a little comfortingly domestic noise.

Gingerly, I remove the urn from the box and carry it through to the sitting room, tucking it into the crook of one arm as I turn the door handle and push the door open with a dry creak of its hinges. I put the casket of ashes on the coffee table between the two sofas, which face each other conversationally. I pause for a moment and consider putting Dad's photo on the table beside the urn. But no, that would be too public an admission of what has gone before, even with the picture of the magpies covering the guilty secret, as in the past. And it would also be too shrine-like. I can see Liz's wry smile, as if she's mocking the idea. I pull the creaking door shut behind me, but then hesitate and open it again, pushing it ajar. It feels more companionable this way. And, yes, I do realise how silly this is and that I'm making a huge issue out of what merely amounts to a jar full of dust. But since there's nothing I can do to bring Liz back, our last threads of connection – no matter how tenuous they may be – have become vitally important. I can't ask her for the truth about her relationship with my father. I can't scream my anger at her for her betrayal. I can't tell her that she's wrecked my life, turning everything I thought I knew about my childhood into an empty charade. I can't weep on her comforting shoulder, emptying out the muddle of conflicting emotions that has been one of her legacies to me. All I have is this last gesture of grudging respect.

I go back to bed, ignoring the now quiet kettle with its wisp of silent steam and shivering a little despite the warmth of the July night. I slip back under the covers, pulling up the light quilt. Lafite, disturbed by the movement, wakes and stretches, then jumps down and stalks soundlessly out of the room, no doubt off on some nocturnal hunting expedition as I hear the clatter of the cat flap moments later.

Pity. I'd have liked his company in the darkness that stretches between me and the dawn.

Chapter 10

Celebrations and jubilations – that's the last shutter finished! At last I can cross that off my to-do list.

I've left the heavy ones that flank the doorway until the end and now they are neatly sanded, undercoated and painted and are resting on the trestles to dry. I'll ask the Thibault brothers to put them back on for me tomorrow. All the windows are now framed with the sage-green panels and I pause for a moment on my way back to the house to survey my handiwork. Most satisfying.

I'm cleaning both the brushes and my green-spotted hands at the kitchen sink when there's a tap at the door and a faint '*Coucou!*' I turn, and am delighted to find Mireille on the doorstep.

'I've come to inspect all the work that's been going on here – both yours and my sons',' she grins, her eyes bright as a bird's in the leather-brown folds of her face.

'Well, you're just in time for tea, too,' I reply.

'Good, I hoped that might be the case.'

We go out on to the terrace, where Pierre is passing roof tiles up to Cédric. Raphael and Florian are elsewhere this week, finishing up other jobs before their break.

'The building inspector is here,' I call, and the men pause in their work.

Peering down from his scaffolding perch, Cédric says in mock alarm, 'Oh, *mon Dieu*, not that one! She's particularly difficult.' He climbs down to join us. His manner has always been nothing but professional when any of his brothers are around, but today I sense that he's been a little more distant with me and it's as if our moment of intimacy at the festivities last night never happened.

The boys explain to their diminutive mother what they've been doing and she squints up at the newly rebuilt chimney and the surrounding roof with a critical gaze, before finally giving their work a nod of approval. 'We're still waiting for the cowl for the chimney. It's on order at Lacombe and will only be in at the end of the month, but as it's summer Gina won't be lighting any fires, I think,' says Cédric. Our eyes lock and I blush at his words as, unbidden, a sudden vision enters my mind of a roaring fire on a winter's night, the two of us sitting in front of the flames sharing a bottle of wine, his lips on mine . . .

'And there's still the internal plastering to be done,' he continues, but his gaze is still focused on my face and I feel even more flustered at the thought that he may be reading my mind. 'But we'll come back after the holiday to finish that off.'

I snap back to reality and try to concentrate on the discussion once again.

'Are you going to use wet plaster or plasterboard?' Mireille asks knowledgeably. I have no idea what the difference is, but I'm thankful to have such unromantic practicalities to focus on in order to banish inappropriate thoughts about her son from my head.

'Plasterboard, as it's easier and quicker. We can fix it between the beams and you won't be able to see the difference once it's painted,' Cédric replies.

'Well,' says his mother somewhat doubtfully, 'if Gina is happy with that solution . . .'

'I'm happy with whatever you recommend,' I say to Cédric, pulling myself together and trying to sound as brisk and business-like as possible. 'Plasterboard sounds fine. And I'm really so grateful to your sons for all the work they've done,' I continue, turning back to Mireille. 'I know it's taken them away from other jobs. Now, let me go and get the tea things.'

I carry the tray out and Mireille and I sit at the table while the brothers perch on the terrace wall. 'We won't stop for long – we need to carry on, to be sure of getting the tiles finished by Friday,' Cédric says.

I've made Pierre his usual tiny cup of strong black coffee, which he downs in one gulp, breaking off for a second from sending a couple of texts to do so. Mireille raises her eyebrows in surprise as Cédric accepts a cup of tea, and then shoots him a sharp glance. 'Aha, I see you've managed to civilise one of my sons at least, Gina.'

Cédric grins and takes a couple of sips, but then stands up and nudges Pierre. 'Come on, Casanova, back to work.' Without thinking, I reach out to take his cup from him and our fingertips brush as he passes it to me. We exchange a smile, the distance that I'd sensed between us closing in a flash. And I only realise how intimate this gesture must look when I catch sight of Mireille, who is watching this momentary exchange like a hawk, an expression of suspicion dawning in her wise old eyes.

But, with her customary kindness, she chooses to ignore my obvious confusion at the fact that she's noticed this English hussy flirting shamelessly with one of her married sons, and turns the conversation to last night's revelries.

'So, did you enjoy our Bastille Day celebrations, my dear?'

I hesitate, another pang of guilt at the memory of exactly how much I'd enjoyed one particular moment in the company of a certain married son of hers preventing my reply. Pulling myself together, I say, 'Very much indeed. You rarely get a community coming together like that in England. At least, the part I come from. It was fun. And you made all us foreigners feel very welcome.'

'*Ah, oui*, the second occupation, we call it. The first dates back to Eleanor of Aquitaine, when this whole region belonged to the English kings. The second has happened a little more stealthily and a lot more recently. But we like having the English here. Everyone knows they make an important economic contribution to the region, especially when times aren't easy. And now with *la crise* in the wine industry, it's even more important. Bordeaux isn't yet as badly hit as some other parts of France, but it's difficult all the same.'

'I know it's getting harder to sell French wine in Britain,' I say, 'but surely the winemakers of Bordeaux can easily sell their production in France?'

'Not so much these days.' Mireille shakes her head.

Cédric, pausing in the act of handing up another stack of tiles to Pierre, chips in, 'It's not cool for the younger generation to drink wine these days. Whisky and beer are much more in.'

'Yes, and the French government isn't very supportive of the wine industry,' Mireille adds. 'In fact, there's a big campaign against alcohol in general, because people are worried about the effects of drinking too much. But they're going to the opposite extreme, so the traditional French way of having a glass or two of wine with meals is dying out.'

Cédric starts up the ladder, a bucket of mortar in hand, but he pauses to call down, 'Yes, it's incredible. Wine is one of France's greatest commodities and yet the wine growers are being left to struggle. You've worked in the industry all your life, Gina, but do you really know how hard it is on the small *domaines* where they have to do everything themselves – grow the grapes, make the wine and then try to sell it too?'

I bridle a little and retort, 'Well, I know it's hard, but the producers need to get their act together. Your country has sat back and let the New World run away with the market.' Normally I'd be backing France to the hilt, but something in his challenging tone makes me defiant. I'm not about to be subjected to a lecture as he mansplains my life's work to me.

'Ah, yes, but isn't the wine-drinking public much the poorer as a result? There'll be far less choice if there's no room for the smaller producers who bring individuality and character to the industry.'

I try to keep my tone level. 'You really don't need to lecture me about French wines. I've spent the last ten years of my life defending your corner. It just feels like France is fighting a losing battle at the moment.'

He balances against the scaffolding and holds up his hands in mock surrender. 'Okay, okay, I'm sorry. We need more people like you in the world to fight for us,' he teases. But then continues in a more serious tone, 'You know, you should write about it, Gina. You understand how difficult the situation is becoming. You could help spread the word, tell people what's really happening in France. Wasn't your father a wine writer?'

Mireille must have heard that from Liz, of course. What else did Liz tell her about Dad, I wonder . . .

'You know, Cédric,' Mireille calls up to the roof, where now only her son's boots are visible as he lies on a ladder across the newly mended area to fix more tiles in place, working methodically up towards the apex, 'you should take Gina to visit the Cortinis. They can tell her more about the situation and show her their vineyard. It's one of the best around here,' she adds, turning back to me. 'Château de la Chapelle, just over in the next valley near St André.'

I recognise the name.

'That'd be interesting. I loved their red, which Cédric intro-duced me to last night.' I marvel at how calmly I manage to say this.

Cédric peers down from the roof. 'I'll get in touch with Robert Cortini when we get back from Arcachon,' he says, his tone concili-atory now. 'In fact, we'll probably see him while we're at the *bassin*. He's usually there at this time too.'

'Robert and Thomas are the sons of the château owner, Patrick Cortini,' explains Mireille. 'Patrick's getting on a bit now, but he still keeps an eye on the *chai*. Robert looks after the vines and Thomas does sales, but all three of them make the wine together.'

'I'll look forward to meeting them in August.' I tell Mireille about the Master of Wine course. 'I need to know a lot more about the technicalities of winemaking,' I finish.

She nods approvingly. 'It sounds like a tough course. But there's not much the Cortinis don't know about wine. They've been in the business for five generations. They'll be pleased to help you, I'm sure. And they're always delighted to meet anyone who's as passion-ate about wine as they are.'

As I say goodbye to Mireille at the kitchen door, she gives me a searching look. And then, nodding back to where her sons are working at the other side of the house, she says, 'You know, Gina, of all my sons, Cédric is the most practical. He's not a great one for showing his feelings – he is a man, after all. But that's how he expresses them – by actions, not words.' She's deadpan, her expres-sion neutral, and I sense she's treading carefully, trying to tell me something important.

I wonder what she's getting at and then, to my shame, I realise that of course she's picked up on the strong current of attraction that flows between me and her son. She probably saw us together last night too. So she's warning me off, in the gentlest and politest way possible.

I blush and try to deflect the guilt I feel by saying, 'I'm so grateful to all your sons, Mireille. I really appreciate the effort they've made for me; I know they've gone out of their way to help. You've all been so kind. I'm very lucky to have such wonderful friends and neighbours.'

'Ah well, we have all grown very fond of you, you know, Gina.' A yellow school bus comes into view in the distance. 'And now here come Luc and Nathalie. I'd better be going.'

'How many grandchildren do you have in total?'

'Nine,' she replies proudly. 'Raphael's four, Florian's three, and Cédric's two. Pierre has none yet – at least, so far as we know!'

'And what is it that Marie-Louise does?' I ask.

Mireille looks a little surprised – perhaps she thinks it's a bit of a cheek for me to be asking about Cédric's wife when I've just spent a good half hour apparently flirting with him over tea on the terrace. 'She's a legal assistant in the *notaire*'s office. It's a pretty demanding role.'

'It must be hard juggling work and family,' I say.

'Well, yes, but of course we all help out. That's what family's for, after all.'

And with that she heads for home.

◆　◆　◆

On Friday afternoon, the Thibaults' white lorry pulls into the courtyard. All four brothers have come to dismantle the scaffolding. Raphael inspects his younger siblings' work with a critical eye, and finally pronounces it to be '*Pas mal*'. It looks a lot better than *pas mal* to me. They've put a layer of new tiles underneath and then painstakingly cleaned the old tiles that were undamaged in the storm, slotting these back in place over the new ones to make a perfectly snug, watertight covering, still weathered in subtle shades of terracotta and cream, so that the restored area blends with the rest of the roof. They've also cleaned off the moss from the remaining sections and replaced several cracked tiles (and I'm sure that wasn't on the original remit). They sweep up the debris that's accumulated under the scaffolding and collect the sheets of plastic and pallets that the new tiles were encased in, leaving everything neat and tidy.

'Can I offer you a drink to celebrate the end of the job and the start of your holidays?' I say.

'*Non merci*,' replies Cédric 'We must get the lorry back to the yard and unload everything. And then go home to pack. Although Nathalie has had her bag packed for two days already, Luc will take a little more organising, I suspect.'

I suddenly realise how much I'm going to miss having them around.

And yes, of course I do mean one of them in particular.

We shake hands as they leave. Cédric hangs back until last, and there's an awkward moment where I extend my hand and simultaneously he leans in to kiss my cheek.

There's that unmistakeable jolt of heat between us again.

Politely ignoring the fact that I'm flushing bright red, he says, '*Au revoir*, Gina. I haven't forgotten about your visit to Château de la Chapelle. I'll be in touch when I get back and have had a chance to organise things with the Cortinis.'

'Thank you. I'm looking forward to it very much.'

The deep-etched lines around his dark eyes crinkle in that sexy smile again. 'And I'm looking forward to seeing you again very much, too,' he replies.

Which wasn't what I'd said at all, actually, I realise, when I replay the scene in my head afterwards, over and over again.

Chapter 11

It's hot. Each day starts with a tantalising hint of coolness in the air and a few faint wisps of cloud in the sky, but these soon evaporate. The geraniums blaze brightly in their pots in the courtyard and on the terrace wall, reinvigorated by the long drink of water I give them each evening and a few hours' respite from the baking sun. But even at this time of day the background hum of cicadas underlies the fluting descant of morning birdsong, before the insects build to a frantic scream that drowns out every other sound and thought.

The heat becomes unbearable by midday, and in the garden leaves wilt and curl, their vitality drained. The grass is bleached to straw. Only the surrounding vines remain as abundantly and exuberantly green as ever, their strong roots able to penetrate to the very heart of the underlying limestone, which holds water like a giant sponge. Perfectly formed bunches of grapes are starting to ripen beneath the neatly trimmed canopy of leaves. Overhead, a buzzard floats languidly in the white-hot sky, its nonchalantly lazy air not fooling the furry creatures that huddle terrified in the grass below as its shadow passes.

Beaten into submission by the unremitting glare of the sun, I move indoors into the twilight of the house where I've closed all my newly painted shutters in an attempt to keep the air here a little cooler.

I decide to pop down to the supermarket and spend a leisurely hour pushing a trolley around the air-conditioned coolness. Once there, my eye is caught by a flutter of red, white and blue bunting and I find myself in that far-flung outpost of Her Majesty's Kingdom of the British Isles: the British Aisle. Bedecked with Union Jacks, on closer inspection the items on offer are mostly curry sauces and taco shells, although Marmite and custard powder are also represented, constituting an interesting reflection of English cuisine through French eyes. But imagine my delight when, sandwiched between the mango chutney and the hot 'n' spicy salsa, I spot a cache of chocolate HobNobs! I scoop up several packets and throw them in with the oozing cheeses, a watermelon and several bottles of mineral water that I've already selected. It's always important to have a balance in life, after all.

In fact, it's too hot to eat much, but I make salads of the big misshapen tomatoes that I buy in the market each week, the concentrated tang of their red flesh dazzling my taste buds. I scatter torn leaves of peppery dark-green basil over them and sop up their juices with chunks of crusty bread, accompanied by slabs of pungent cheese.

After lunch, I have a siesta, something I've never done before in my life. But in this heat it's almost impossible to move until about four o'clock, when the sun's rays begin to lengthen and soften just a little. So I lie on one of the battered plastic loungers in the shade or, when it's too stiflingly hot to be outdoors at all, on the bed in the spare room, where it's cooler and there's an intact ceiling. Sometimes I read, but more often I just lie on top of the covers, listening to my music. And usually I sink into a deep, dreamless, heat-drugged sleep. I know it won't help the night-time insomnia, but at least it's one way of catching up on my sleep deficit. At first

I feel guilty about indulging in a midday nap, but I soon realise there's nothing to feel guilty for – it's not as if there's anybody around to judge me, nor anything else I should be doing.

I've ordered some of the books I need for the Master of Wine course, so occasionally the bright yellow van of *La Poste* appears up the drive to deliver another parcel. It's a daunting reading list.

As well as the theory, there'll be practical exams to assess my tasting skills and my knowledge of world wines, but I've had a lot of opportunity to taste wines from far and wide in my buying career, so it's just going to be a question of keeping up to date and making sure I've covered some of the less common regions and wines. I know Harry will help me with this – he's remained in touch and offered support. And I can always ask Annie for help when it comes to the New World. She's now working for the company that bought out Wainright's.

The other sections of the syllabus look as if they're going to be a lot more taxing. There's a whole section on the production of wine, which includes such topics as the chemical composition of grapes, pests and diseases and the intricacies of fermentation. I managed to scrape a pass for GCSE chemistry but that was years ago and I can't say anything at all has stuck. There'll be two three-hour exam papers on this section. And then I need to know about 'The Business of Wine', which includes a section on financial and commercial awareness, so my finely tuned understanding of accounting and economics (ha!) will be brought into play here. And finally there's a topic entitled 'Trends and challenges facing wine-producing countries and regions'. And as I'm rapidly discovering, there's enough material in Bordeaux alone to fill the whole of the three-hour exam paper on this one, let alone what's going on in the rest of the wine-producing world.

Every time I look through my well-thumbed copy of the syllabus, I feel completely overwhelmed. How could I ever have imagined I'd be up to this course? There are about three hundred Masters of Wine in the world. I used to think this was a lot. But now I realise it's a tiny number. It feels as if I'm trying to join an extremely exclusive club, and I'm very much afraid they're not going to want me for a member. Through my doubts, I can hear Liz saying, 'Go on, Gina – give it a go! Who knows where it might take you.' And Dad saying, 'You can do it. You're as good as anyone else. Anything that's worth doing is a challenge.'

I feel like retorting, 'Go away. I'm not talking to either of you right now.' But the most annoying thing about people who are dead is that you can't tell them what you think of them.

Supposing I do actually manage to pass all four exams and the practical tests too, I then have to produce a ten-thousand-word dissertation. And in this heat I can hardly summon the energy to lift my head from my pillow. But it's going to be a long winter, stuck here in France I suspect, and maybe by then I'll be glad to have so much work to keep me busy.

One afternoon, I'm rudely awoken from my midday nap by the ringing of the phone. I've been so deeply asleep that it takes a second or two to register that it's Annie calling.

'Hi, hon, how are you? My God, were you asleep? Sorry to wake you up. But how decadent at this time of day, while some of us are slaving away. I'm just ringing to see what your plans are in the next few weeks. Are you completely snowed under with visitors?'

I contemplate the lonely days and nights stretching ahead and reply that I have precisely nothing in the diary.

'Oh, good. Well, can I come and stay? I thought I'd pop over. I'm dying to come and see where you are and have a proper catch-up.'

I'm wide awake immediately, delighted at the prospect. 'Come whenever. Stay as long as you can. Oh, Annie, I can't wait to see you!'

Hooray. Company at last. And it's my age. And it speaks English. My spirits lift and I feel a much-needed surge of energy coursing through my listless limbs as I begin to plan for her visit.

◆ ◆ ◆

I stand outside the customs shed at Bergerac airport at the back of a small crowd of people waiting to meet friends and loved ones off the Stansted flight. Most of the crowd are English and several have brought along their dogs, who are busy trying to sniff one another's behinds, winding their leads around the legs of anyone who gets in the way. The odd volley of barking breaks out when the sniffee takes exception to the overly enthusiastic attentions of the sniffer. Strange, this habit of bringing animals to the airport, lending it the charmingly whimsical air of a village dog show. I've only ever seen it here at Bergerac, so maybe it's a particularly British expat thing.

I peer into the gloom of the arrivals hall, from which people are now beginning to emerge, trying too hard not to look self-conscious as they are met by a sea of expectant faces and breaking into relieved smiles when they find the one they're searching for. I'm looking for a sultry brunette, this being the last guise in which I saw Annie, so am caught off guard when a curvaceous platinum blonde steps through the door and begins waving at me enthusiastically. I should have known. She was sure to get back in touch with her inner blonde before too long.

I've been feeling a bit of trepidation about Annie's visit. While we're very good friends, it has dawned on me that we've never actually spent such an extended period of time together, sleeping under the same roof. There was that time we went to Vinexpo, of course, back in the boom years when Wainright's was thriving and Harry was feeling particularly flush. We stayed in a B&B in Bordeaux for three nights, spending the days tramping through the halls of the vast exhibition centre that hosts this world wine event every other year, and the evenings at restaurants along the *quais* in the city centre. But that doesn't really count. It's not the same as having someone staying with you in your own home.

However, the minute I see Annie tottering towards me in a pair of perilously high strappy sandals, an oversized pair of sunglasses pushed back on top of her bright crown of hair, wheeling her large suitcase behind her and grinning from ear to ear, I know it's going to be fine. We hug, already simultaneously talking and laughing, and I help her drag her case to the car.

She loves the house, exclaiming enthusiastically at the setting, the space and her pretty room. I've moved back upstairs to let her have the spare room. The ceiling above my bed is still a rough cross-hatch of wooden laths supporting the roof tiles and a neat new silver lining of insulating material. It gives the room an industrial air, but at least it's weathertight, if a little stuffy in this heat. I've taken to keeping my make-up in the fridge after my mascara melted into a sticky black mess and leaked all over the dressing table.

Once she's unpacked, we sit on the terrace in the balmy evening air and Lafite, curious at the arrival of this newcomer, jumps into her lap and begins purring loudly as she strokes his furry head. I open a cold bottle of Clairet, which Annie pronounces 'yummy' (a technical term us highly trained wine tasters like to use), and leans back in her chair, stretching luxuriantly.

'God, look at my awful pasty arms compared to yours,' she says. 'I've definitely got some serious work to do to lose this London pallor in the next week. You look wonderful, Gina, if a bit on the skinny side. Your new life in France obviously agrees with you.'

'Well, it's not as if I've got a lot on my plate at the moment. No job, no man – it's the secret of a stress-free life. Or rather, no life at all. So I've been able to put in a good deal of sunbathing time of late.'

'Yes, but I'm full of admiration for you making a start on the MW course. It's something I'm always meaning to get round to but there's never the time. It's bloody difficult too – not sure I could handle it at all.'

'But then you've got a very full-time job. How is business these days?' I ask.

'Pretty dire actually, between you and me, but I'm lucky to be in work at all so I shouldn't complain.'

'I know,' I sigh. 'I was in the wrong area really, on the French side.'

'I do admire the cussedness of the French, though. They certainly don't believe in making life easy for themselves and you have to give them credit for caring so passionately about their winemaking. It's just that the New World is good at manufacturing wines that suit what people are looking for – cheap and cheerful, uncomplicated, accessible. A bit like what a man looks for in a woman really, now I come to think of it. Speaking of which, what's the local talent like here? Any sexy French gentlemen callers?'

There's no way I'm going to admit to my sadly delusional passion for Cédric, which Annie would pounce on like a cat on a field mouse if I gave her the faintest hint of a clue.

I say airily, 'Well, unless your taste runs to oily estate agents who've seen the back of fifty, then not really. Although I have been hotly pursued by an English guy recently.'

'Well, that sounds promising,' Annie replies, delighted at the prospect of some juicy gossip. 'Tell me more!'

'Yup, his name's Nigel and he has a comb-over. Oh, and he's desperate to share the inner workings of his septic tank with me. That really is about as good as it's got.' I mentally cross my fingers, lying through my teeth and trying to banish from my mind's eye a sudden image of Cédric's face crinkling in that smile of his, which never fails to make my breath catch. I continue firmly, 'I'm afraid you've come to the wrong place if you're in search of a week of holiday romance. There's been a definite drought of late, and I'm not just talking about the weather.'

'Well, it's high time you came back to Britain and your Auntie Annie will have to see if she can't come up with someone. I'm sure I can find a suitable candidate in my little black book.'

'No, thank you,' I say firmly. 'And anyway, I'm still off men after the whole Ed saga. How does that old joke go? What's the difference between a man and a catfish?'

'I don't know, what is the difference between a man and a catfish?' Annie dutifully replies.

'One's a scum-sucking bottom-feeder. And the other one's a kind of fish.'

She cackles appreciatively, then frowns. 'Rubbish! Never mind fish. It's just like riding a horse. You have to get straight back in the saddle. Or so I understand. Not that I've ever ridden a horse . . .' And our conversation descends into the sort of raucously hilarious girl chat I've so been missing.

At the end of the evening, light-headed and light-hearted from a potent combination of friendship, wine and laughter, we finally say goodnight and Annie, weaving slightly, disappears off to the guest room clutching a large bottle of Evian. As I shut the back door for the night, I realise the cicadas have finally gone quiet, perhaps giving up in the face of such shrill competition from the terrace.

In the velvety darkness, the faint hoot of an owl drifts across the newly fallen silence.

◆ ◆ ◆

Next morning, putting the kettle on to boil for a much-needed cup of coffee to get the day started, I discover we're out of milk. *Merde*. Never mind, some croissants would be nice too, so I jump in the car and nip down to Super U before there's any sign of life from Annie.

I get back to find her clattering mugs in the kitchen. She's wearing shorts and flip-flops, the straps of a bikini showing under her camisole top.

'I've fed Lafite,' she says, gesturing to where he's crunching the last few morsels in his bowl. 'Such a honey, he spent the night curled up on my bed.'

'Huh, what a tart that cat is,' I retort.

'Oh, and someone phoned,' she continues. 'A French bloke. Trouble is, he was talking so fast I couldn't make out half of what he said. Something about *une heure*. So I think he's going to call back in an hour's time. Or maybe at one o'clock, Anyway, he'll definitely call back.'

'Okay. Probably the stonemasons,' I reply, hoping I sound nonchalant. 'They're due back from holiday about now so they're probably phoning to arrange when they're coming to finish fixing the upstairs ceiling.' I don't want to admit to myself how much I'm looking forward to seeing Cédric again. And there's absolutely no way I'd admit it to Annie, whose finely honed sense of smell isn't limited to wine tasting. She'd be on to any whiff of a possible scandalous affair like a rat up a drainpipe.

I busy myself pouring the milk into a jug and putting breakfast things on a tray. 'Shall we have this outside?'

'Lovely. I'm planning on spending every possible second in the sun today. Have to get some serious tanning in.'

'Well, I hope you've brought the factor 50. You'll be needing it by midday, or you'll end up with a truly British dose of sunburn,' I laugh.

After breakfast, we spread ourselves out on the sun loungers. Annie's brought copies of all the latest English magazines with her so we settle down in our bikinis, with Aretha singing her heart out on the speaker and *Vogue, Harper's* and *Hello!* scattered around us.

After a while, she puts down her magazine to re-baste her skin with suntan lotion and turn on to her front. 'You know what you were saying last night about French wines?' she says. 'Are you seriously telling me local producers in Bordeaux, the sacred heartland of the industry in France, are making New World-style wines these days?'

'Yup,' I reply. 'You can taste them if you're interested.'

'Love to. You know me – I never rest in the diligent pursuit of something new for my discerning clients. You know my theory about good wine being like good sex. So, in the absence of any chance of a holiday romance, bring on the wine!'

I shove my feet into my flip-flops – the terrace paving is now scalding hot – and go indoors to retrieve a selection of wines.

We spend a happy hour tasting the line-up of six bottles I've arranged on the table and comparing notes. I'm glad Annie agrees with me about these local wines. They're a real find.

By nine thirty, we've made inroads into most of the bottles. Even though we've only sipped the wines, the growing heat has made them go straight to my head and I feel happy and relaxed with my friend at my side. My tongue loosened, with a little encouragement from Annie, I launch into a diatribe against men in general (and Ed in particular), raising my voice over the music that blares from the speaker.

'. . . And that is why I'm not the slightest bit interested in being in a relationship.' I'm really getting into my stride now and my voice has become a bit shouty, but I don't care. 'Even if there was anyone around these parts who was remotely attractive. Men are completely unreliable, IMPOSSIBLE BASTARDS!'

And then, to my absolute horror, I glimpse a movement from the corner of my eye and realise that we're not alone. Cédric and

Pierre have just rounded the corner of the house carrying a long ladder between them and are now standing dumbstruck, surveying the scene in front of them. And, oh, dear, I have to admit it doesn't look good. How much of my rant did they hear?

I grab my cotton shirt from the back of the sun lounger and hastily pull it on. Annie, still blissfully unaware of their presence, waves her wine glass in a toast to my noisy declaration of independence, her ample curves overflowing her bikini.

Pierre is now grinning from ear to ear, while Cédric, who's carrying a large cement cube as well as his end of the ladder, looks somewhat bemused.

'Oops!' Annie says cheerfully, catching sight of the two brothers but not at all abashed. 'Didn't realise we had company.' And she bounces across the terrace – bounce being the operative word – to shake hands.

'*Bonjour*, Gina,' says Cédric, turning to me and taking my awkwardly proffered hand too. He holds it in both of his for a moment or two and our eyes lock, his gaze seeming to ask a question and mine, I'm sure, about to give away the hunger and longing I feel at the sight of him. I drop my eyes to hide my agitation. 'I'm so sorry – we didn't mean to disturb you. We did knock at the kitchen door but I don't think you could hear us.'

No, well, I suppose we were making a bit of a racket. One of us in particular, anyway.

'I phoned earlier,' he continues, 'to let you know we'd be coming round in an hour's time. The cowl for the chimney has arrived.' He nods at the cement block, which he's put down on the ground beside the ladder.

'Ah,' I nod, meeting his gaze again in what I hope is a dignified, calm, cool and collected manner, despite my state of undress and the fact that I'm in the company of a similarly scantily clad female, surrounded by discarded clothes, magazines and enough bottles of wine for quite a respectable party at ten o'clock on a weekday morning. 'So that was the message. It got lost a little in translation, I'm afraid.'

I can't help thinking he's looking incredibly handsome after his time away – tanned and more relaxed than usual. And then, to my added confusion, I realise he hasn't relinquished my hand and I'm in no hurry to relinquish his either. A realisation that immediately makes me drop it, as if it's burning as hotly as the flagstones of the terrace or my own flaming cheeks.

'How was your holiday?' I ask.

'Great, thanks. We had a good time. Nathalie and Luc loved being at the beach with all their cousins so it was very easy. And Marie-Louise's father has a boat at the *bassin* so we had some good outings in it. Do you sail?'

'Yes, I love it,' I reply. 'Though I haven't been for years. I used to go with my father when I was young.'

'Well, you'll have to come along sometime,' he smiles.

Great, I think, pulling at the hem of my shirt and wishing it covered more of the flesh of my legs. That'll be a fun outing, sitting in your wife's father's boat and lusting after her husband. But I smile and nod with what I hope looks like enthusiasm.

'You seem to be a little – er – occupied . . . Would you like us to come back another time?' asks Cédric. 'It'll only take a few minutes to fix this on top of the chimney.'

Annie's grasp of French is pretty slender, but she clearly gets the gist of this last bit. 'Oh, don't mind us,' she says cheerfully, with another wave of her wine glass. 'Please carry on.'

'Yes, do go ahead,' I say. 'I'll just clear a bit of space for the ladder.' I scoop up an armful of clothes and magazines and scurry inside where, thankfully, I pull on a skirt and smooth down my hair, trying to regain a little composure.

I come back out into the bright sunshine. Pierre is holding the ladder while Cédric climbs up, carefully balancing the heavy cowl as he goes. Annie, not the least abashed, is perching on the terrace wall, rather coquettishly it has to be said, looking on appreciatively.

When Cédric descends a few minutes later, Annie gestures to the bottles of wine on the table. 'Would you like a drink?' she asks. 'We were just tasting some very good local wines.'

The two brothers clearly find the invitation hilarious. 'It's good that you enjoy them so much,' says Cédric, trying to keep a straight face, 'but *non merci*, we have to get to another job. There's a lot to do as we're just back.'

'Please excuse us,' adds Pierre, still grinning broadly at Annie, 'but Raphael is a slave driver and he'll already be wondering where we are. Another time perhaps . . .'

As they pick up the ladder ready to leave, Cédric turns to me. 'We'll be back in about two weeks' time to finish the work on the ceiling upstairs. I'm afraid we're a bit busy catching up with work after the holidays at the moment, so it can't be any sooner. I'll phone you to give you better warning next time though,' he says, with a roguish glint in his eye. 'Oh, and one other thing. I saw the Cortinis at the *bassin*. They'd be delighted to show you round at Château de la Chapelle and let you taste their wines. They suggested we visit on Friday evening, but perhaps you'd rather wait until your friend has departed? Although she'd be very welcome to join us if it would be of interest.'

'That's so kind. I'm sure you'd love to come along, wouldn't you, Annie? She's in the wine business so she might be a good contact for them.'

'Okay, great. I'll come and pick you up about five thirty then.'

They load the ladder on to the back of Cédric's pickup and disappear down the drive.

Back on the terrace, Annie is sitting at the table in the shade of the sun umbrella, awaiting my return. 'Well, well, well, Miss Peplow,' she crows gleefully. 'You *are* a dark horse. Why didn't you tell me about the hunky French workmen?'

'I don't know what you mean,' I retort haughtily. 'They've just been doing the repair work here. Their mother is my neighbour. They've been very kind and helpful, that's all.'

'Oh, come off it!' she scoffs. 'I haven't seen so much chemistry since my science teacher dropped a whole jar of sodium into a sink full of water.'

'Why,' I ask, seizing the opportunity for a diversion, 'what happens when you drop sodium into water?' Sometimes Annie surprises me with the things she knows.

'Let's just say the results are pretty explosive,' she replies. 'But don't go trying to change the subject. What's going on between you and that good-looking older brother?'

'Precisely nothing,' I say firmly. 'He happens to be happily married to a gorgeous French wife and has two lovely children to whom he is utterly devoted.'

'Well, he wasn't behaving like someone who's entirely happily married. He couldn't take his eyes off you. He definitely fancies you – there were about forty thousand volts of electricity between you when he was holding your hand. And don't tell me you don't fancy him back. I know you, Gina Peplow, and you're absolutely hopeless at lying, so don't even bother trying.'

'Okay, okay,' I hold up my hands in defeat, plonking myself down on a chair beside her and reaching for one of the open bottles of wine. It is about time for elevenses, after all. 'Despite my earlier ravings about men, I do like him. Very much indeed. He's not only gorgeous, he's also got a great sense of humour and is a wonderful father to his kids. His family all think the world of him and he's practical, hard-working and reliable. And I get the feeling he likes me too. So he's absolutely perfect, apart from the teeny-weeny little matter of his wife. There's no way I'm having an affair with a married man, especially one whose mother is my friend and neighbour. I know how devastating it is to be on the receiving end of being cheated on and there's no way I'd want to be responsible for inflicting that kind of pain on anyone else. His children are wonderful – you just couldn't hurt them. And his wife's actually really nice too . . .' I trail off lamely.

'So if his family life's all so perfect, why does he look at you like a starving man who's just caught sight of a Big Mac and fries?'

'Please,' I laugh, 'at least credit me with being something a little more classy than the equivalent of a trip to McDonald's.'

'Okay then, a starving man in a Michelin-starred restaurant. Whatever. The French are supposed to be far cooler about this sort of thing. Perhaps he's looking for a *ménage à trois*. A sort of *Vicky Cristina Barcelona*. Only set in Sainte-Foy-la-Grande.'

'Doesn't have quite the same ring to it somehow, does it? And I'm not the slightest bit interested in being part of anything like that if it is the case. Which, anyhow, I strongly doubt.'

'Ah, the eternal triangle,' says Annie sagely. And then, lightening up, she says, 'Now, enough about the men in your life. Or *not* in your life, as the case might be. Let's get back to the serious business of tasting these wines. Where were we before we were so opportunely interrupted?'

I pull the cork from the next bottle and, speaking of love triangles, think of Liz's lonely life, wondering for the umpteenth time what exactly her role was in my parents' relationship.

Pulling myself together quickly, before Annie's uncanny powers of observation detect another secret that I'm keeping from her, I slosh some red into our glasses. 'Right then, see what you think of this.'

Chapter 12

Promptly at five thirty on Friday evening, Cédric's dark-blue pickup pulls into the courtyard. He jumps out and comes to knock at the door to the kitchen, where I've been hovering for the last half hour, trying to pretend I'm busily engaged in various domestic tasks. The sink and its taps, under the window, which is – coincidentally – the best vantage point to look out at the courtyard, are gleaming I've cleaned them so thoroughly, and now I'm scrubbing my hands to try and get the smell of bleach off them again.

My heart gives a little lurch at the sight of him. He looks freshly scrubbed himself, in jeans and a neatly ironed shirt, the sleeves rolled up to show a length of muscular, tanned forearm. Trying hard to suppress a surge of unruly lust that suddenly makes me very conscious of every part of my own body, I open the door with a gracious and composed smile. For once I've had time to prepare and so at least I'm a bit more elegantly groomed than on many of Cédric's previous visits.

He kisses me hello, most decorously of course on either cheek, but nonetheless it occurs to me that it's the first time he's done so when we're alone. Oh, God, how sad am I? It's just the French equivalent of shaking hands, for heaven's sake, and I'm being completely pathetic.

'I'll just go and see if Annie's ready,' I say brightly, my voice sounding, to my guilty ears at least, unnaturally high and nervous.

She's in her room, putting the finishing touches to her make-up. 'Is he here? Oh, good.' She looks at me appraisingly and reaches out to brush my cheek with her thumb. 'An eyelash,' she explains. 'But other than that, you'll do. You scrub up quite nicely, you know. Now let's go get him!'

'Annie,' I say firmly. 'We're not getting anyone. And especially not him. He's out of bounds.'

'Okay, okay, whatever you say, Little Miss Celibate. Just seems like a bit of a waste to me, that's all.'

I glare at her sternly. She makes a zipping gesture across her lips. 'Not another word, I promise,' she says, still grinning broadly, obviously relishing the prospect of watching me squirm.

She clambers into the narrow back seat of the pickup, displaying a good deal of brown thigh and just a hint of bottom-cleavage for the benefit of Cédric, who is politely holding the door open for her. Isn't there a golden rule about not displaying so much flesh when you're approaching the age of thirty? If there's not, there should be. Although that still wouldn't stop Annie from flaunting it shamelessly.

Somewhat more decorously, I hope, I climb into the front passenger seat, and Cédric closes the door and comes round to jump into the driver's seat. I can't help noticing his capable hands on the steering wheel as he starts the truck and we pull away. Oh, God, concentrate, woman! I catch a glimpse of Annie's twinkling eyes, looking at me from the rear-view mirror.

'So, Cédric, tell us about the Cortinis. Have they owned Château de la Chapelle for long?' I ask airily, determined to maintain a businesslike tone.

'Yes, for several generations. Patrick, who is the father of Robert and Thomas, owns the château now. His grandfather came from Italy to work there at the beginning of the last century and he ended up marrying the owner's daughter. Hence the Italian surname. So the property's been in the family one way or another for hundreds of years. Patrick's nearly seventy now, but he's still very involved in the winemaking and keeps a close eye on the boys. Robert, who was in my class at school, is in charge of the vines, and Thomas, who's two years younger, does the marketing. Eventually Patrick will hand over to his sons, but he finds it hard to stop. His wife left him about twenty years ago and so the château and the wines have been his whole life ever since. Keeping busy stops him from getting lonely, I suppose.'

Annie, who's hanging over the back of my seat to listen to the conversation, asks me to translate this last bit. 'Blimey,' she says, 'who'd she leave him for? Most women would love to be married to a château owner. It doesn't get much more romantic than that!'

'Sadly, winemaking's not a very romantic existence in reality,' replies Cédric. 'As you probably know, it involves brutally hard work, long hours and low returns. Madame Cortini got fed up with it all in the end and once the boys left school she went off with a dentist from Bordeaux, who was a much better proposition. She's been far happier with her new life ever since. Not that the boys see that much of her nowadays.'

So much for the fairy-tale life in a castle then. Modern-day princesses take a far more pragmatic approach, it would seem.

'Robert's married and has three kids, the same age as Luc and Nathalie and then one a bit younger,' Cédric continues. 'Thomas is still a bachelor, though – he spends a lot of time on the road trying to sell their wine.'

I can almost see Annie's ears pricking up at this last bit of information and she raises her eyebrows at me in the mirror. I'm not sure whether she's interested on my behalf or her own but either way, the prospect of an unattached male of around our age has got her attention.

Steadfastly ignoring this diversion, I firmly guide the conversation back to the safer ground of the wines they make and the production methods they use. Cédric, his attention fixed on the traffic, which is quite busy at this time on a Friday evening, even on these little country roads, professes not to know that much about the technicalities. 'But here we are,' he says, swinging the pickup into the driveway of Château de la Chapelle, 'so you can ask the experts.'

It's a pretty *domaine*. The driveway, which runs up the slope of the hill, is flanked by an avenue of dark green cypresses and beyond them on either side the rows of vines run in precisely parallel lighter green lines, their tops neatly trimmed to a uniform height. Just visible beneath the leaves nestle the clusters of ripening grapes, their black skins softened to shades of velvety purple-grey by their fine coating of bloom.

We park in front of the house, an elegantly proportioned building. The hillside dips slightly behind it and then rises again, forming a natural bowl that is perfect for the cultivation of vines. On the skyline sits a little stone church with a tall, pointed steeple. 'That's the chapel of Saint André, from which the château takes its name,' explains Cédric, pointing it out.

We walk round the side of the house to a yard where a large tractor, towing a fearsome-looking trimmer whose blades glint in the evening sun, is being effortlessly reversed under the roof of a lean-to shed for the night.

'There's Robert,' says Cédric, raising a hand in salute. 'Good timing – it looks like he's just finished for the day.'

A stocky, compact man in a green boiler suit climbs down from the cab and the two men greet each other with the hug and double kiss that still seems so foreign to us more cold-blooded Brits. Then

Robert turns to greet us, wiping his hands on the cotton of his neat overalls before shaking ours.

'Come into the *chai*,' he says. 'My father and Thomas are inside, I think.'

In the gloom of the vast shed, the walls are lined with gleaming stainless-steel vats. A pair of legs clad in an immaculately pressed pair of khaki trousers protrudes from the small door in the front of one of these and a muffled stream of expletives can be heard echoing off the walls inside it.

Cédric and Robert grin at one another and Robert turns to Annie and me. 'Excuse me for one moment,' he says, and walks across to tap the legs. There's a brief pause and then a renewed outburst of cursing, louder than before. 'Papa,' Robert perseveres, 'we have company.'

The legs back out of the vat and Patrick Cortini emerges fully, a handsome elderly man with a shock of white hair and a thick white moustache. His face creases into a delighted smile at the sight of us and he comes over to shake hands.

'What charming young ladies,' he beams, gallantly declaring himself '*Enchanté*' to make our acquaintance. 'Please forgive me,' he says, 'but some idiot hasn't cleaned out the *cuves* properly, so I'm having to do them again myself. We're getting everything ready for the harvest in a few weeks' time and as usual it's up to me to make sure everything's done right.'

Robert continues to smile serenely, even though this dig is clearly aimed at him and his brother. He turns to us and says calmly, 'Actually, the *cuves* are perfectly clean, but Papa finds it impossible to admit that anyone else is capable of doing anything properly.' He gives his father a fond hug. 'Still, it keeps you out of trouble, I suppose.'

A slightly younger and taller version of Robert materialises from an office in one corner of the *chai* and Cédric introduces us to Thomas.

'So you are in the wine trade?' he asks in English, with a very charming French accent.

'Well, I used to be, but not now. Annie, however, is a buyer for one of the biggest chains in the UK,' I explain.

'But Gina is an expert too. She is currently doing a course to get some higher qualifications,' adds Cédric, laying a hand lightly on my back as he speaks. I feel a glow of pleasure at his approving glance and supportive gesture.

'In that case, it is an even greater pleasure to welcome the two of you to Château de la Chapelle,' Thomas smiles. 'Shall we show you round the cellar first and then we can go and taste the wines?'

It's a well-run operation. Annie and I have visited enough wineries in our time to be able to spot signs of sloppiness or taking shortcuts and there are none here.

Patrick proudly shows us the nuts and bolts of the cellar: the gleaming, surgically clean steel vats, the vast yellow Vaslin press, the de-stemming machine and assorted pumps and long coils of plastic tubing, stowed in the corners for now but ready for action when the hectic days of harvesting begin next month. They show us the bottling room, where the machinery stands quiet for the moment amid orderly metal cages of filled bottles, waiting to be labelled and have the capsules put over their corks when orders come in. And they usher us through to the hallowed coolness of the barrel cellar, where the previous year's wine rests quietly in softly scented barrels of French oak, taking on the wood's subtle flavours for a final twist of finesse and smoothness.

Our tour finally over, Thomas leads us to the back of the house, where a shady terrace gives on to the vineyard. We sit down at a table spread with a checked cloth and Robert tells us about his work in the vines. 'We practise *culture raisonnée*, using as few pesticides and chemicals as possible and encouraging the vines to find their own balance and strength. It's not quite organic, but it's reassuring to have the treatments to fall back on if necessary – for example, if we have a cool, damp summer, like last year, when mildew can become a problem and threaten the harvest. But you will know all this already, of course,' he smiles at us.

Thomas adds, 'People in Britain tend to ignore the fact that French wine is often a more natural product than its non-European counterparts. And of course, wine from Europe has less far to travel than New World wines, so it's a far greener product with a much smaller carbon footprint. These things are becoming more important, I think, and we need to get the message across.'

Patrick has disappeared into the house and emerges carrying a tray laden with glasses and bottles. Thomas leaps up to help his father, deftly opening the two reds to let them breathe a little before we begin with the whites. They're delicious – an un-oaked Sauvignon Blanc with just a hint of Sémillon to soften and balance the acidity, and a more complex oaked wine, heavier on the Sémillon, made in a more sophisticated, almost Burgundian style. Then there's a crisp Clairet, the perfect wine for a hot summer's evening with its mouth-watering cherry flavours. And finally we taste the two reds, the medal-winning oaked version and a simpler un-oaked one. They're really well-made clarets, smooth, fruity Merlot with a tantalising edge of spicy Cabernet Sauvignon.

Annie seems to be seriously interested in the wines and Thomas gives her a bundle of tasting notes, technical details and prices. With a flourish, he adds his card to the pile of literature. She picks it up and examines it. 'Thanks,' she says. 'Sorry I haven't got any of my cards with me. But I'll pass this on to my colleague who handles Bordeaux. It's just a shame it isn't Gina any more these days.'

He passes me a card as well. 'Give us a ring any time if we can be of assistance with your studies.'

It's very pleasant indeed sitting on this beautiful terrace talking to these knowledgeable and charming men, but reluctantly I realise it's half past seven and they will no doubt all be wanting to get home to their families and their Friday night suppers. Cédric has been quite quiet during the course of the evening. A few times I've caught him watching me when I've glanced surreptitiously at his face in the shadows, where he sits listening to the Cortinis as they talk about their wines and occasionally asking Robert about his work in the vines or enquiring after his family. Their easy friendship is obvious and they hug again fondly when we say goodbye. Old Monsieur Cortini plants enthusiastic kisses on the cheeks of his female guests and urges us to come and visit him again whenever we feel like it.

Cédric drops us back at the house, declining our offer of a further drink. '*Merci*, but we're having supper at my mother's house tonight. Another time perhaps, though,' he says. And do I imagine it, or is the look he gives me especially tender?

Obviously I don't imagine it as, the minute he's gone, Annie turns to me with a gleeful grin. 'Well, you've certainly made a huge impression there, Gina Peplow. He couldn't take his eyes off you all evening!'

'Old Monsieur Cortini, you mean? Yes, well, I am particularly attractive to septuagenarians, even if I do say so myself,' I say, in a vain attempt to deflect her.

'Bollocks, Gina, you know I'm talking about Cédric. He's besotted with you. He went to all that trouble to take us over there and bring us back. He didn't need to be there at all. Probably just looking for an excuse to throw his awful harpy of a wife off the scent and spend an evening with you!'

'Don't say that,' I wail in despair. 'She's truly, honestly not like that at all. She's really lovely. I don't know what's going on, but I have to say I actually think the less of him for it. Honestly, what hope is there if even the most decent seeming, well thought of, caring men behave like this?

'I'm sick of it all,' I continue bitterly, working myself up to a fury that surprises even me. 'Lies, deception, cheating. It's grubby and hurtful and . . . and wrong!' I finish up somewhat lamely.

And I realise I don't know whether I'm talking about my situation or my mother's, whether I'm angry with Cédric or with my father and Liz. But one thing's for sure: I can choose not to be part of anything like that. And that's what I'm resolved to do.

◆ ◆ ◆

On the last night of her holiday, Annie takes me out to dinner at a restaurant on the banks of the river, looking back across the stretch of dark water in whose depths the lights of Sainte-Foy gleam like a school of golden fish. As we walk in, a man at one of the tables stands up and says '*Bonsoir.*' It's Robert Cortini, who shakes hands and introduces us to his wife, Christine. 'It's our wedding anniversary,' he explains, 'so we thought we'd treat ourselves.'

'Congratulations,' I reply. 'Have a good evening.' And we make our way to our table at the other side of the room, leaving them to their meal.

'Isn't it nice when you start recognising people when you are out and about?' says Annie. 'You must really be starting to feel like you belong.'

And I realise that she's right. It's as if this place – and the people in it – are quietly weaving silken threads, as fine as a spider's web, that are beginning to bind me here.

We settle down with the menu. Once the waiter has taken our orders and deposited a basket of bread on the table before us, along with the bottle of chilled white wine that we've chosen, Annie reaches over and takes my hand. 'Gina,' she says seriously, 'we need to talk.'

'Oh no,' I say in mock despair, 'are you breaking up with me?'

'Of course not, I'd never do that,' she smiles. 'But I am worried about you. You've stuck yourself away down here in the depths of France in that lonely house with only a cat for company. You're not sleeping. And you're not eating properly; you're getting far too thin. And I couldn't help but notice that casket on the table in the sitting room. I know it's none of my business, but I've got a strong suspicion it's not for keeping your secret stash of chocolate HobNobs in. It's not healthy, you know, Gina. Having some time on your own is no bad thing, but you seem to be cutting yourself off completely. I know it's hard for you to trust again after what Ed did to you, but you're too young to turn yourself into a lonely cat-loving spinster with the remains of a dead person for company. Honestly, it's like something out of a Hitchcock movie; you're going to go potty and start murdering people. And don't expect me to come and stay again if you do.'

I give her a watery smile, swallowing back the sudden tears that spring into my eyes. I know I'm pretty close to the edge, struggling to make sense of what my life's become. And when she leaves tomorrow, I'm going to be cut adrift again, floating aimlessly on an ocean, the solid ground of the life I used to know – or thought I did, at least – having disappeared beyond the horizon. I hadn't realised my fragile state was so obvious. I thought I'd been doing a good job of keeping up the appearance of normality.

'It's like I said before,' Annie continues, 'you've got to get back in the saddle. Get out there again and meet somebody. Why don't you come back to England? You can stay on my sofa bed while you look for a job. I know it's not the easiest of times, but maybe I can help you find something in the wine trade. Or you could write, like your dad did.'

'Oh, Annie, that's kind of you, but I'm honestly okay here. I want to get the Master of Wine course under my belt and the studying will keep me busy in the autumn, plus a few trips back to England along the way. And I really do need some space at the moment. There are a few things I need to get sorted out in my head. Yes, admittedly, I do have my aunt's ashes in my sitting room, and I know that's not the most normal state of affairs – or even legal – but it's only until I decide what to do with them. I just need a bit of time.'

She lets go of my hand to allow the waiter to put our starters down in front of us, and tucks into an oyster, washing it down with an appreciative slurp of wine.

'Well, okay, I'm going to give you 'til Christmas. But if you aren't looking better by then – and if you still have mortal remains sitting on your coffee table – then I'm coming over here to forcibly remove you. Deal?'

'Deal,' I say, laughing and holding my hands up in mock surrender. 'Don't worry, I'll be fine.'

'Well, in my opinion you'll be fine a lot faster if you have a bit of good old-fashioned hot sex. I know, I know,' she forestalls me as I try to interrupt, 'I'm not saying it has to be with the gorgeous, perfectly compatible, thoroughly nice-seeming man who is obviously keen on you and whom you clearly like in return. Good grief, that would be making life far too easy, after all!'

'Apart from the very serious complication that he's married with children,' I butt in.

'Well, yes, there is that,' she concedes with a sigh. 'But what about Thomas Cortini? He seems to be unattached. Didn't you like him? You've got his number – phone him up and say you want to come and give his sales strategy the once-over. Or you need him to explain the ins and outs of malolactic fermentation. Or you'll come and help him with his next bottling run. Whatever. Think up some spurious excuse and make a move. That's what I'd do in your shoes.'

'Shh, keep your voice down, his brother might hear,' I hiss, with a nod across the room to where Robert and his wife are tucking into their main courses. 'And anyway, I don't fancy Thomas Cortini,' I protest.

'Don't you? I thought he was cute. But in any case, that's not the point here. He may not necessarily be the one, but he may be able to introduce you to his other single friends. You have to make an effort, Gina, because men aren't just going to come marching up your drive.'

'Actually, you're wrong there,' I say with an airy wave of my hand. 'Men seem to be always doing exactly that. Just not the right ones. But I do take your point and I promise I'll make an effort. Anyway, let's just enjoy our meal. Now, tell me, what's on the agenda for when you get back . . . ?'

After our meal, we emerge into the warm night air and wander across the bridge spanning the broad river, making our way back to the car. We stop beside one of the tall pillars covered with ivy and baskets of coral-pink petunias and lean on the parapet to gaze at the gold-flecked water flowing beneath us.

'This is a beautiful place,' murmurs Annie dreamily.

Perhaps it's the wine making me maudlin, but I'm suddenly overwhelmed by a feeling of loneliness. 'Oh, Annie, I'm going to miss you so much.' I lean my head on her shoulder for a second. 'Thank you for being such a good friend.'

'*Bonne nuit*,' says a quiet voice beside us and we pull apart and turn to see Robert and Christine Cortini, who are walking across the bridge arm in arm.

'Good night,' we say. 'We hope you had a good evening.'

They nod and smile, continuing on their way, and we follow in their wake a few minutes later, driving home, under a sky filled with stars, in comfortable silence.

Chapter 13

The house is very quiet after Annie's gone, leaving behind her a pile of sun-crinkled, suntan-lotion-smudged magazines and a faint whiff of her perfume.

The August heat continues day after day and, despite the odd rumble of thunder carried on the thick night-time air now and then, there's no rain. By the end of the month even the vines are starting to look parched, the green rows dusty and a few leaves starting to bleach and fall. It's perfect weather for finishing off the ripening of the black Merlot and Cabernet Sauvignon grapes though, concentrating the flavours and sweetness into the promise of a full-bodied, heady vintage.

I've grown so used to the quiet company of just an old black cat and my own thoughts that I jump out of my skin when the chirp of the telephone suddenly breaks the silence one morning, almost tripping over the threshold as I dash inside to answer it.

It's Cédric.

I smile into the handset, expecting him to say he and Pierre will be along tomorrow to finish putting up the plasterboard. And so I'm disproportionately disappointed to hear him explain that Raphael has had an accident and they won't be able to come for several more weeks as they are now busy covering other jobs.

'I'm *so* sorry,' I say with heartfelt sincerity. 'I hope Raphael is okay. Was it serious?'

'A stone fell and crushed his hand. An occupational hazard in our line of work. He has a broken wrist and two fingers were quite badly damaged. But he's tough and it'll mend. It's going to take a while, though, and we're very behind with several jobs that we need to get finished before the autumn. I'm really sorry, Gina, but we have to prioritise. I hate to leave you in the lurch though. Are you doing all right on your own?' He sounds so sincere that, for a second, I'm tempted to tell him the truth. That I'm struggling. That I'm lonely. That I'm in desperate need of company. And that I'd prefer his company above all others. I'm overwhelmed with a sudden yearning for him, for his kindness, his solid, capable presence. His friendship.

I realise that I've come to value him as a friend, even if being anything more than that is impossible. But I bite back the words as he continues, reminding myself that he's just being professional.

'If you like, I can give you the number of a plasterer who might be able to come and finish the work for you sooner.'

'That's okay,' I reply. 'It's not urgent, after all. I can live with it for now. I'll wait until you can do it, if that's all right.' And I'd rather have you here than anyone else, I manage not to add.

'Once the weather changes, we'll have more time for indoor work. I'll call you. And I really am sorry, Gina.'

Not half as sorry as I am, I think as I put down the phone. I wander back to the terrace and pick up my book, the enticingly entitled *Concepts of Wine Technology*, whose complicated chemical formulae I have, quite literally, been sweating over.

I sigh and put the book straight back down again, feeling disappointed and disgruntled.

And then a small rectangle of card that I've been using as a bookmark catches my eye. Thomas Cortini.

I hear Annie's voice urging me to call him up on some pretext or other. My heart's not really in it, but hearing Cédric's voice on the phone has reminded me how lonely I am and the prospect of the empty weeks stretching away before me suddenly makes me crave company. I look up, gazing absently at the view beyond the garden. Of course! The harvest is rapidly approaching, judging by the darkly ripe grapes on the vines all around me. I'll volunteer my services as an extra pair of hands. Despite my career in the world of wine, I've never actually worked a harvest. This is the perfect opportunity to learn a whole lot more about the detailed intricacies of winemaking first hand. And it should be far more interesting seeing it done for real rather than trying to read about it in a book.

'Gina, how good to hear from you.' Thomas's voice is genuinely warm. 'How are you? Annie has returned to England now, I suppose? You must be missing her. The harvest? Why yes, if the current weather holds, we'll be starting on the whites next week or the week after. It's been so hot and dry the grapes are slightly small, but in wonderful condition. We'd be delighted to have another pair of hands in the *chai*. I'll call you when we have a confirmed date, but *en principe* it'll be a week next Monday.'

◆ ◆ ◆

I'm surprised at how cold it is at six thirty in the morning. Until now the days have still been beautifully warm, but then I'm not usually up this early. I nip back into the house and grab a fleece jacket before jumping into the car and driving to the Château de la Chapelle to report for duty. 'Come about seven o'clock,' Thomas instructed me yesterday. I'm early, eager to create a good impression on my first day. As I drive into the yard, I'm surprised to find it already a hive of activity.

The vast doors of the winery stand open and the bright lights inside throw a sharply defined rectangle of illumination on to the white dust before the entrance. A conveyor belt has been positioned just inside and at the far end the de-stemming machine waits, silent for the moment. A pump sits underneath it and a long stainless-steel tube runs from here to the top of one of the lofty metal tanks. Thomas and his father, perched on the metal walkway suspended above the *cuves,* are heaving the far end of the heavy pipe into position above the vat's open lid.

'Ah, here is our new helper. *Bonjour*, Mademoiselle Gina!' calls Patrick, and he picks his way down the ladder-like stairs to come and greet me. Thomas follows behind him, having fixed the pipe in place.

'Gina, thank you for coming to help,' he smiles. 'Let me introduce you to Jacqueline, our assistant in the *chai*.' A stocky, cheerful-looking young woman emerges from the office. A gleaming golden tooth embellishes her friendly grin, giving her a faintly piratical air.

A tractor pulling a large, deep-sided trailer behind it swings into the yard and I glimpse Robert at the wheel. He reverses neatly, precision perfect as he lines up the back of the trailer with the end of the conveyor belt.

'Come on,' says Jacqueline. 'We're on the sorting table. You stand on that side.'

Robert jumps down from his cab and opens a round hatch in the end of the trailer while Jacqueline attaches a plastic pipe to an outlet on the underside to capture the juice that is already starting to run from the bunches of golden-green grapes. Catching sight of me, Robert comes round to say hello, then reaches back into the cab of the tractor to flick a switch. The trailer's internal screw mechanism begins to turn, disgorging its load in a steady stream on to the belt, which Jacqueline has set running. She hits a button on the de-stemmer and another on the pump and the machinery leaps into action with an ear-splitting din.

Thomas appears at my side. 'Take out any large sticks and leaves, and any bunches of grapes that don't look good,' he shouts above the noise. I nod, concentrating hard on the moving belt before me and trying to pick through the heaps of fruit as nimbly as the other two. I find it hard to follow the fast-moving stream and rapidly begin to feel queasy with the movement and the noise and the fact that I didn't really feel like eating any breakfast at such an early hour this morning.

Jacqueline grins across at me, waving a hand to attract my attention. 'Gina, are you okay? You've gone as white as a sheet. Don't try to follow the motion of the belt. Fix your gaze on one point, like this. That's better. You'll find it easier now.'

Actually, there isn't much debris to remove at all. The grapes are beautifully ripe, with no signs of mildew or rot, and there are just a few leaves and the occasional woody bit of vine to take out. The bunches of fruit then fall through the de-stemmer, which spits the stems into a bin, the loosened grapes pouring into the hopper of the pump, where they are seized by the machinery and fired through the long pipe into the gaping mouth of the vat.

At last the stream of fruit coming out of the trailer dwindles and then stops and Robert nimbly switches off the screw, shuts the hatch and disconnects the hose from underneath, before hopping back into the cab and driving off for the next load. The last grapes drop into the pump and Thomas hits the off switch on the machinery, leaving us standing in sudden silence, the only sounds the soft dripping of juice into the vat and the ringing in my ears.

'Let me show you the control panel for the *cuves*,' offers Thomas, leading the way to an efficient-looking array of lights and buttons fixed to the *chai* wall. 'Five years ago we replaced our old *cuves* with thermo-regulated stainless-steel ones, so we can control the temperature in each from here. The white grapes need to be kept cool to preserve the very delicate flavours of the fruit – that's why we start picking them so early, before the sun begins to warm them up – so we're chilling the vat they're going into. We're starting with the Sauvignon Blanc and it's vital to keep the grapes cool if you want to capture those elusive elderflower and gooseberry notes in the final wine. We'll easily finish the Sauvignon this morning and then change over vats to begin the Sémillon.'

I nod. 'Who's picking the grapes?' I ask.

'We use a local contractor, Benoît Michel. All our grapes are machine harvested nowadays. The technology is so good now it doesn't harm the vines the way some of the old *vendangeurs* used to. And this way we can get our grapes in at the very best moment, when they reach optimum ripeness. So we have just two people working in the vines today, Benoît driving the *vendangeur* and Robert bringing in the trailer-loads of fruit. The turnaround is very efficient.'

And right on cue we hear the tractor manoeuvring the next trailer into position at the end of the sorting table. We hurry back to our positions as the stream of green-gold fruit starts to pour on to the conveyer belt and the machinery roars into action once again.

Two trailer-loads later, Christine Cortini appears in the doorway, a large wicker basket over one arm. She does the rounds, greeting each of us in turn, and then busies herself in the office. A delicious aroma of percolating coffee wafts in our direction.

Suddenly, I realise how cold my hands and feet are from standing on the cement floor at the sorting table, my fingers and the cuffs of my sleeves stickily damp with a mixture of chilly grape juice and dew. The last of the batch of grapes trundles along the conveyor belt, then rattles into the de-stemmer and the fruit cascades into the pump. Jacqueline nips round to hit the off buttons on the machines and gestures towards the office with a tilt of her head. 'Coffee time.'

I rinse my hands and then rub my neck, which is beginning to ache, trying to roll the stiffness out of my shoulders. I glance at my watch. It's not even ten o'clock and I feel like I've done a good day's work already.

Christine is pouring hot, strong coffee into cups and hands me one. I clasp my hands around the small cup to warm them, wishing it was a large British mug with a generous slug of hot milk added. But in my cold, tired state, the shot of scalding, tarry liquid is the best cup of coffee I've ever drunk. The men come in from the vines, Benoît shaking hands all round, and the whole team stands around the desk drinking coffee and munching flaky croissants, which Christine produces from her basket. Patrick, who has been everywhere this morning, darting from sorting table to trailer to *cuve*, and even popping out into the vines to supervise activities there, is euphoric about the quality of this year's harvest. 'A wonderful year, even better than 2005, you'll see. Gina, you'll be able to boast to your friends that you have had a hand in making some of the finest wines of the century!'

'And the century is still so young,' remarks Thomas drily. 'But then, according to my father, every vintage is one of the best ever.'

'It is going to be an outstanding year though,' says Benoît (another thick *sud-ouest* accent for me to try to decipher). 'Especially for the reds. I've never seen such clean Merlot. And the Cabernet Sauvignon is going to be superb. Perfectly ripe.'

'Yes, as long as we don't get thunderstorms next week,' says Robert, shaking his head. 'A downpour at this stage and in this heat can rot the grapes overnight. With the sudden rain they can swell and split,' he explains to me. 'You can even get hail some-times, which is disastrous. All that work and care throughout the year and then you can lose the whole lot just before the harvest. *Vignerons* don't sleep well at the best of times, and at this time of year hardly at all.'

'Pah!' exclaims Patrick. 'Don't you worry – we'll get the harvest in all right. And just you wait and see. It's the vintage of the cen-tury, I tell you! Right, back to work, everyone.'

Robert already has another trailer-load of grapes waiting for us, so we get straight back to it. Revived by the break, I sort the fruit with new energy and am gratified to notice that my fingers are now working almost as fast as Jacqueline's across from me. The coffee has warmed me up and the sun is beginning to heat the air outside the entrance. We work on cheerfully for another hour and then the rhythm of our work is broken as Robert announces that that's the Sauvignon Blanc finished and they're about to start bringing in the Sémillon.

As he drives off with the trailer, there's a flurry of activity in the *chai*. We have to change over to another *cuve*, which involves repositioning the huge metal pipe. Thomas nimbly climbs up on to the walkway in the roof and manhandles the top end, while Jacqueline and I wrestle with the bottom. There is a series of joints in the piping, each closed with a strong metal clip, and we have to release these to swing the steel tubing round to reach the new vat. I strain to undo one clip, scraping my fingers and breaking a couple of nails, while Jacqueline competently manages the others. We get the pipe into position just in time as Robert arrives with the next trailer-load.

I hurry back to the sorting table, where the belt is already running, and focus once again on the fast-moving stream of grapes.

On the dot of midday, silence falls again as Thomas switches off the machines. We've filled one tall vat with Sauvignon Blanc and half-filled its neighbour with larger, yellower Sémillon grapes. 'Lunchtime,' says Jacqueline with gusto. 'Christine cooks for everyone during harvest so it'll be good. It's on the terrace.'

In the loo, I catch sight of my reflection in the mirror with horror. My hair is wild, coming out of the elastic I've tied it back with and sticking out in strange wisps where I must have pushed it back with hands covered in grape juice, a natural but not very becoming alternative to hair gel. I wash my hands and face and let my hair down, tucking the band into my pocket for later. As we step out on to the terrace, I blink in the midday sunlight and peel off my jacket to let the rays warm my aching shoulders. At a trestle table set with a check cloth, Christine is setting out baskets of bread and plates of pâté. Suddenly, I realise I'm absolutely ravenous, despite the mid-morning croissant.

'*Bon appétit*,' smiles Christine as she pulls up a chair. Patrick pulls the corks from two bottles of Clairet and tours the table, filling glasses with the pomegranate-coloured wine.

Thomas offers me the basket of bread and I smear a crusty chunk of baguette with rich, garlicky pâté. 'How have you enjoyed your first morning?' he asks.

I chew and swallow. 'Good,' I reply. 'Hard work, but I was expecting that, and very interesting. It's great feeling you're part of the process that leads to something as wonderful as this.' I raise my glass. 'And I still find it magical. You take all those trailer-loads of grapes and turn them into bottles of wine. It's a kind of alchemy.'

Thomas smiles. 'You're right. Even after all these years, we still find it miraculous too. And you never really know what you're going to end up with until the final blending and bottling. There's a saying around here that red wine is made on the vine and white wine is made in the *chai*. Each has its own particular challenges.'

Robert chips in from the other side of the table, 'Yes. This year we've been lucky with the weather, but there's still lots to do before the wine is in the bottles and we can start to relax a little.'

Patrick is now handing round a platter of pork chops and he deposits a huge slab of the golden, fragrant meat on my plate. 'Here you are, Gina, we need to feed you up ready for an afternoon's hard work.' Christine follows in his wake, cradling a steaming bowl of fried potatoes, encrusted with dark flecks of sweet-smelling garlic. I pile my plate high. I'm not sure whether it's the good food or the fact that a meal eaten in company is so much more appetising than the solitary snacks that I've grown accustomed to at home, but I seem to have got my appetite back. A green salad moistened with the tang of mustard vinaigrette follows and then a white wheel of creamy Camembert. The last crusts of bread are used to wipe plates clean, as Christine pours us each a small black coffee to round off the meal. I drink mine thankfully, needing an antidote to the comfortable blanket of drowsiness the food, wine and sun are weaving over me.

Suddenly I hear the words '. . . *Thibault frères* . . .' and I tune in to a conversation Robert and Christine are having with Benoît and Jacqueline.

'Marie-Louise says Raphael's hand is still quite bad,' says Christine. 'It's taking a long time for the break to mend. But it doesn't stop him turning up on site to tell them they're not doing the job right!' The others chuckle appreciatively.

'What are they working on at the moment?' asks Jacqueline.

'The church at Les Lèves,' replies Robert. 'They won the contract to redo all the stonework, including the bell tower. It's a massive job. Short-handed as they are, they're going to battle to finish it on time. They're working straight through every weekend at the moment.'

Suddenly, my bedroom ceiling seems a total embarrassment. I now appreciate fully what a favour Cédric and his brothers have done me. And how much clout their diminutive mother must have over her strapping sons to have persuaded them to help me out in the first place. I'm beginning to wish I'd taken up Cédric's offer of the contact details of a plasterer. I'm quite sure finishing off the work on my roof is a complete nuisance for them and they're just too polite to say so – or too afraid of Mireille. But at the same time I feel a pang of longing for Cédric's company and a sense of profound sadness at the thought that, once the work on my house is finished, I won't have any excuse to see him again. I keep quiet, feeling ashamed and deflated, and take another sip of my coffee. The others down theirs and push back their chairs.

Robert and Benoît leave the table first, heading out into the vines for the next load. Back in the *chai,* the sides of the two steel vats we've been filling are now covered in droplets of condensation up to the level of the cooling grapes and juice within. We work on steadily and by five o'clock we've filled three *cuves* with white grapes.

'Good work,' enthuses Patrick as he inspects the temperature control panel's winking lights.

At the end of the long day, I'm bone-achingly tired. The restorative effects of lunch have worn off long ago and there's been no stopping for a British-style tea break in the afternoon. And now we have to hose down the equipment, taking apart the de-stemming machine and rinsing every grape skin and stalk out of its honeycomb drum. Then we clean the pump and all the tubing, spewing residue on to the *chai* floor. This then has to be scraped up using a long-handled rubber blade and shovelled into bins. Finally, the cement floor has to be hosed down and the water scraped into the drain that runs down the centre of the *chai*. At last, at six o'clock, peace falls as Jacqueline turns off the pressure sprayer and I scrape away the last drops of water.

'*Impeccable*,' declares Patrick.

I am now so tired I can hardly speak. I ache all over and my head feels heavy and dull from trying to follow the rapid-fire colloquial French spoken by my colleagues in such strong accents. I'm cold and damp and hungry.

It's the best day I've had in ages. And tomorrow I'll be back to do it all again.

Chapter 14

The first week of the harvest passes in a blur.

The highlight of each day is the lunch break when we all gather on the terrace for another of Christine's delicious, and seemingly effortlessly prepared, meals. It's not just the good food and the welcome chance to sit down in the sun-dappled warmth for an hour or so. I find myself slowly starting to feel included, a fellow worker and one of the team rather than just a curious foreigner who's popped along to play at winemaking for a day or two. I've tuned in to the personalities of the group and the rhythm of the work in the *chai* and no longer feel like a clumsy outsider as I learn the steps to the whirling waltz of the wine harvest. Finally, instead of just reading about it in books, I'm joining in the dance. And at the same time I realise I'm becoming part of a community here; maybe even building myself some new foundations after feeling unsettled for so long.

Each night I soak my aching limbs in a hot bath and then collapse wearily into bed. Once I was so tired I even fell asleep in the tub, the cooling water jerking me back to consciousness as it lapped around my stiffening shoulders. And I sleep better than I have done in ages. The combination of physical labour, hearty meals and stimulating company is a healthier diet than I've had for a long time.

◆ ◆ ◆

The unmistakeable scent of fermentation begins to percolate through the *chai*, a fruity yeastiness that hints at the extraordinary changes that are taking place in the vats of grape juice. And most days Sylvie Clemenceau, the oenologist, comes by to discuss the results of the latest tests that have been carried out on samples from each of the *cuves*. Patrick and Thomas call me over the first day she arrives.

I take to her immediately. Her wide brown eyes and mop of curly hair accompany a smile as warm as the early autumn sunshine outside the *chai* door. Her manner tells of a quiet competence, as she patiently explains each step of the testing process and the results for my benefit.

'So it's as we would expect after such a hot summer: the sugar levels are very high, which is going to translate to higher alcohol levels in the wine than normal. Rather like many reds from the New World that are grown in hot, sunny climates. There's also a greater risk of the fermentation stopping before it's complete, so we'll have to watch for that. We may need to use different yeast. We will need to filter later on. And we'll probably add a little more of the press wine than usual to the free run. The blending is going to be critical to make sure we get the balance right.'

'Fortunately, Gina has an excellent palate,' says Thomas. 'We'll include you when it comes to the blending stage,' he says, turning to me.

'In the meantime,' offers Sylvie, 'if you'd like to come and spend a morning with me in the lab, you'd be very welcome. I can show you exactly how the samples are tested and how we obtain and record the results.'

'I'd love to,' I reply. 'That'll be a huge help in trying to understand some of the chemistry.' I turn to Patrick and Thomas. 'If the Cortinis can spare me, that is?'

Patrick smiles. 'Well, it'll be a loss, but we'll let you have a morning off once we start pressing the Clairet. For once, the weather is on our side this year.'

◆ ◆ ◆

And so a few days later I present myself at the little laboratory in Saint André-et-Appelles for a morning's apprenticeship. It's a very different place of work, a tiny pair of rooms with clinical white walls, although everything is as scrupulously, almost surgically clean as the equipment in the *chai*. When I arrive, Sylvie is talking to a winemaker who has come to hand in some samples. 'Come on through,' she says once he has departed, and she shows me to the little lab behind the reception room. Crates of sample bottles are stacked high, each one neatly labelled. 'As you can see, it's very important to be systematic and to make a careful note of where each sample is from,' she says. 'Imagine how disastrous it would be if we gave the wrong results back.'

She hands me a white coat. 'Here, put this on. Now you look the part. We'll make a chemist of you yet!'

'Thanks,' I say, 'but I think it's going to take more than a white coat to achieve that.'

We perch on stools at a long counter and Sylvie shows me how she carries out the basic tests. 'For more complex analysis we send the samples to the main lab at Sauveterre,' she explains. 'The turnaround is fast and we can have the results back to each *vigneron* the same day.'

We are interrupted at regular intervals as more samples are dropped off, and at eleven o'clock the driver arrives to collect the batches to be taken to the Sauveterre laboratory.

We pause then for a welcome coffee break. While it's less physically tiring than working in the *chai*, I'm finding it mentally exhausting trying to keep track of the stream of information Sylvie is imparting. I scribble notes frantically. But light is beginning to dawn and it's already far clearer seeing the chemistry in action than my attempts to understand it from the textbooks.

'So that covers the main tests we do at this stage in the wine-making process,' Sylvie summarises. 'And of course the other major round of testing we do is in the spring, to establish whether or not malolactic fermentation has taken place. Let me show you how we do that to give you an idea. I think I have some old duplicate results.' She pulls open the drawer of a filing cabinet and extracts a folder.

'Ah yes, here we are. As you know, we need to make sure that the malic acid has been transformed into softer lactic acid, and this happens during a second fermentation, which may occur in the tank or after the wine has been put into barrels.' She hands me two squares of textured white paper. 'Can you spot the difference?'

I ponder the purple-brown stains on each of the sheets, fading in a spectrum as the paper, exposed to a chemical solvent, has separated out the different constituents of the wine as they soaked their way up to the top of the paper. Finally, I point to the right-hand one. 'This one has a gap, just here,' I say.

'Exactly right,' replies Sylvie. 'What it is showing is an absence of malic acid, which is still present on the other sheet – here, you see? So that is how we know the second fermentation has taken place. We test for something that isn't there, rather than something that is. In other words, we're looking for a negative.'

And suddenly, triggered by her words, my mind catapults off at a complete tangent. An image of the shelves of files in Liz's office flashes into my head. Why didn't I think of it before? A negative. There has to be one. Of the photo of my father. And maybe there'll be others too. Images that will give me more of a clue about the extent and timing of their relationship. Pieces of the nightmarish jigsaw that I'm trying to put together, with most of the bits missing and no idea of the final picture. I can hardly concentrate on the rest of what Sylvie is saying and am relieved when the hands of the clock nudge round to midday and it's lunchtime.

'Thanks very much, Sylvie. It was a wonderful morning, so helpful,' I say as I leave.

I get into my car and head up the hill for home. Lafite, who's been curled up peacefully on a chair in the kitchen, looks up, startled, as I crash through the door, flinging my keys on to the table.

I head straight through to the study, to the bookcase where Liz's files are arranged, each neatly labelled by year. Within them, alphabetical dividers separate plastic sleeves that hold strips of negatives, each marked with a small white sticker giving the name of the subject and the precise date the photos were taken. I work feverishly, going first to the folder for 1980, the year of my birth. I start with the obvious (which would be making things just too simple, of course, but I live in hope), turning to 'P' for Peplow and then 'D' for David. I leaf through the plastic sleeves but find nothing. I need to think more laterally. I turn to 'W' for wine. There are several strips of pictures of wine bottles and barrels, but no picture of my father tagged on to one of these as an afterthought. 1981 is the same. Next I seize the folder marked 1979, the year my parents met, the year of their wedding. I'm certain Liz and Dad didn't meet before this; my mother told me so categorically when I asked why Liz wasn't in the wedding photos, so this is the very earliest year from which the photo could date. I page through again, squinting as I hold strips of negatives up to the light to make sure none of the figures is Dad.

Liz was a professional. She methodically and systematically catalogued every picture she took. Even ones that turned out badly are still here, though they've been scored through with a marking pen. Some of them are amazing. Pictures of fashion models and portraits of film stars leap out at me. But none is the photo I'm looking for. Finally, just as I'm about to give up, I page through the 1979 folder and turn randomly to 'V'. And there it is. *'Vins, Salon, Bordeaux. 22-24 Oct 1979'* in Liz's neat handwriting. My father used to come to these wine exhibitions every year for his work. I pull out the three strips of negatives, holding each up to the window to scrutinise them in the light. There are figures in many of the pictures, but none is my father. I start to slide the strips of film back into their transparent sleeves. And then I stop. Each frame is numbered with its own tiny digits. And between two of the strips, three numbers are missing. I check back through the other pages of negatives. All the numbers are there. It's only on the strip I'm holding in my trembling fingers that three of the frames have been carefully cut off. And I realise I have a result.

Just like the test at the lab, sometimes you have to look for what is missing.

The acid test for a guilty conscience.

◆ ◆ ◆

That night my insomnia returns with a vengeance.

After discovering the missing negatives, confirming that the incriminating photo of Dad was taken after my parents were married, I've spent the afternoon back at the château working in the *chai*. I've lugged equipment to and fro and run up and down the catwalk's steep metal stairs countless times to readjust pipes over the top of the vats. I've wheeled a heavy canister of carbon dioxide gas from one end of the winery to the other, and I've helped wrestle into place the lengths of steel piping to carry the contents of the vats of Clairet to the press, causing a minor disaster when, distracted by the thought of those missing negatives (what *was* Dad doing in the other two pictures?), I accidentally undid one of the joints too early, flooding the floor of the *chai* with sticky pink juice, pips and skins. Clearing up took even longer than usual this evening.

I was too preoccupied to eat any lunch and too distracted to eat supper. Lafite's indignant, hungry meowing finally made me put away the files that I had spread about the study floor, kneeling in the middle of them and looking for more missing negatives. But it seems Liz didn't go to any more *Salons des Vins*. I could find no similar entries in subsequent folders.

So now my head aches from squinting at negatives, my stomach is growling with hunger and yet again I'm wide awake at 2 a.m., my mind buzzing. What have I learned? That the photo of Dad was very probably taken either during or immediately after the wine exhibition back in the seventies. Meaning that it was well before he met and married Mum.

That's one good thing, and it looks as if maybe they didn't spend time alone together again. Although I realise there's no evidence for this. Maybe she just stopped taking photos of him after the first time . . .

I think of the urn of Liz's ashes, still on the coffee table in the sitting room. I'm no nearer to deciding what to do with it. But tomorrow I'm going to shut the door so I don't have to look at it every time I go past. Ha! That'll teach her. Though of course it won't.

Troubled, broken dreams blur the boundaries between wakefulness and sleep, a shifting kaleidoscope of faces and photographs. I dream I'm in the *chai* with Dad and I give him a glass of wine to try from one of the vats. It's a wine I've made myself. I wait with pride, and some trepidation, to hear his verdict. 'God, Gina, this is absolutely dire,' he says. 'What have you done to it?' Furious, I take the glass and taste it myself. He's right. It's off. Sulphurous and stinking. Like wet dog and mouldy rubber. The liquid is murky and covered in slime, like water in a stagnant pond. I look around the *chai* and see Liz pressing buttons on the temperature control panel. 'Hey!' I shout. 'Get away from there!' She ignores me and the lights start to flash a warning, an electronic alarm beeping insistently. And I struggle up, surfacing through the layers of sleep to find my alarm going off because it's time to get up once again and go to work at Château de la Chapelle.

Chapter 15

By the time the last of the Cabernet Sauvignon has been pressed, it's the middle of October. I've been working at Château de la Chapelle for four weeks and the harvest is now over. Across the region, only the occasional harvesting machine can still be seen sailing ponderously up and down the vineyard rows, bringing in the late-harvested Sémillon grapes at the châteaux where they make the sweet wines for which Monbazillac and Sauternes are famous. The bunches are furred with a blanket of noble rot and will be made into a golden nectar that is as mellow as the autumn sunlight.

The final job for us in the *chai* is to decant the fermented and pressed red wines carefully into barrels. Universally acknowledged as the best in the world, the wood comes from ancient forests in the middle of France. Englishmen may lay claim to hearts of oak, but France's heart truly is made of oak and each year she generously sacrifices a little to help finish off the wines that her sons and daughters have laboured so hard to create. The Cortinis replace about a third of their barrels each year, so Jacqueline and I are unwrapping the bulky, curved parcels that have been delivered from the barrel-maker. I love the smell of the wood and stroke the smooth fineness of its grain as I peel off the plastic covers. We roll the barrels into position in the cellar and wedge chocks under each one to hold it in place. Then, closely supervised by their father,

Thomas and Robert connect the pumps and pipes that will lead the wine from the vats into each *barrique*, where it will stay for up to a year while the deep red liquid is suffused with the smooth vanilla flavours from the wood, which help to add depth and balance to the mix of fruit and tannins.

Patrick gently knocks a silicone bung into the top of each barrel. These will be removed at regular intervals so that the levels can be kept topped up to prevent too much air getting in and spoiling the wine.

The barrels exude a delicate breath, filling the cellar with faint perfumes of fruits and flowers. The wines are shaping up nicely, but the Cortinis will only really know what this year's vintage will taste like when the time comes for the final blending next year.

'And now,' says Patrick with a smile, 'we breathe a big sigh of relief and have a small pause.'

'Yes,' grins Thomas. 'Before we have to do it all over again.'

'And of course in the meantime there's the small question of pruning the vines, replacing those that are damaged, replanting the areas that are past their best, ploughing and spraying,' adds Robert. 'Not to mention bottling, labelling and actually selling the wines . . .'

Patrick raises his bushy eyebrows and shrugs. '*Ah, oui*, my dear sons, but that is business as usual in the world of wine. Whatever else could you possibly wish to be doing instead?'

◆ ◆ ◆

In the vineyards bordering my garden, now that the fruit has been harvested, the leaves turn a glorious gold, a final flourish before the vines transform themselves into black, wizened stumps for the winter. Magpies balance on the wooden posts that support the trellis of fine wires on which the vines are trained. Mostly the birds are in pairs (oh, joy!), but occasionally these coalesce into larger groups, fluttering and squabbling as each tries to assert its territorial rights. Distracted from my reading, I count them over and over again as the birds group and regroup and I try not to think of the photo in the silver frame.

At long last, Cédric phones. I've almost persuaded myself that I've stopped wondering when he'll call. I've got used to lying in bed at night gazing blankly up at the silver-covered insulation and the rough laths of the roofing. I've tried hard to push away any thoughts of attraction between us and just about managed to convince myself that I'm so focused on my studies now that there's no room for anything – or anyone – else in my life. But when I pick up the phone and hear his voice, there's a distinct quickening of my heartbeat, and I try hard to maintain an air of calm detachment in my voice as I reply to his questions. Yes, I've been fine; yes, I enjoyed working the harvest at Château de la Chapelle; yes, the studies are coming on fine. And the work on the church at Les Lèves?

'Finished, thank goodness,' he says. 'You'll have to come and see it one of these days. It's turned out well, we think. I'd be pleased to show you what we've done.'

And Raphael's hand?

'Better now, he's back in action. He and Florian are finishing dismantling the scaffolding on the church tower. So Pierre and I can come on Monday morning to get started on the work on the ceiling for you, if that's convenient? We've got a couple of things we need to do in the afternoon, but we should be able to get the job finished on Tuesday morning at the latest. It's not going to take us long.'

'Yes, that'd be fine,' I reply. 'But there's no rush. Come whenever suits you, if you have other work you need to get done first.'

How cool am I?

'No, Monday will be fine. You've been very patient. We'll be there around nine. We need to go to the builder's yard first to get the materials we'll need.'

'Okay, if you're sure. That's great then. Have a good weekend. See you Monday.'

And I sit down at my desk, feeling just a little wistful for something that feels like it's now over. Before it had ever even begun.

◆ ◆ ◆

I'm still glad to see the blue pickup, closely followed by the red motorbike, roll up the drive on Monday morning. I've shut myself away from the outside world since the harvest, politely declining the occasional invitation from Celia to come for lunch or dinner, my only other human contact – apart from sporadic trips to the supermarket – my phone calls to my mother once a week and cheery emails from Annie, full of news and jokes and how busy she is at work. My replies, in comparison, seem stilted and dull. So it's good to have Cédric and Pierre here, for a day or so at least, and to have some noise and activity in the house. Lafite winds himself round Cédric's green overall-clad legs and he crouches to stroke him.

Straightening up, he catches sight of me standing in the doorway and comes to kiss me on both cheeks. 'Gina, it's good to see you again,' he says warmly.

My heart lurches at the sight of him, and my stomach does a double backflip at the touch of the rough skin of his cheek against mine. What is it about this man? I've missed his steady, quietly capable presence, and the way he genuinely listens when he talks to me. Seeing him here again now only serves to make me realise just how lonely I've been feeling.

164

I'm annoyed at myself for being so stupid. Haven't I learned my lesson by now? I'm absolutely resolved not to waste any more time on impossible, unattainable relationships and I reply briskly, with a brightness that sounds brittle to my ears.

'Lovely to see you both. Come on in. You know the way . . .'

They bring in tools, sections of a small scaffolding platform and large sheets of grey plasterboard, and carry everything upstairs. I've managed to push the bed into a corner away from the open area of ceiling that they'll be working on. They quickly cover everything in clean plastic sheeting and set to work.

I discover that I start to feel more light-hearted than I have done in weeks as I hear the two men chatting and laughing easily as they work in the room above me. It's not that I'm needy and weak, just that it's nice having company in the house, I tell myself.

At midday, they come down the stairs. 'Well, we've got the boards up,' says Cédric. 'I'll pop back tomorrow morning to tape the joints and skim them and then the ceiling will be ready for you to paint. It's going to be as good as new when you've finished.'

He busies himself putting tools into his pickup. Do I imagine it, or is he playing for time?

Pierre puts on his helmet and gives a wave as he roars off down the drive, leaving a cloud of white dust hanging in the air behind him.

'We've left the bed in the corner for the time being,' Cédric says. 'Otherwise we'd just have to move it again tomorrow. I hope that's okay?'

'Fine,' I say.

'Gina,' he says. And hesitates, suddenly awkward. 'There's something I wanted to ask you.' He sounds nervous, something I've never heard in him before.

'Yes?' I ask. And suddenly I find I can't swallow because my throat has constricted. With hope? Or is it despair?

'If you aren't busy, would you come and have dinner with me tomorrow evening?'

A bombshell.

It's all I've ever wanted and all I don't. Handed to me on a plate after all these months of wondering, dreaming, hoping. He must see written clearly on my face the conflicting emotions that crowd in as I take on board what he is asking. What he is offering.

It's everything. And nothing at all.

I clear my throat. 'Just to be clear,' I say cautiously, 'who else would be there?'

He looks confused.

'Nobody. Just you and me. We can go wherever you like . . .'

As he tails off, a red rage floods my veins like liquid fire, flushing my face with its righteous heat.

'How dare you,' I say coldly, but my voice is shaking with emotion. 'What the hell is it with you Frenchmen? No, never mind you French – just men in general. You all think you can play games with women. The fact that someone is in a serious relationship seems to mean nothing at all to you. Well, I can tell you, I'm not interested in cheating. I want no part of it. So thank you very much for your terribly kind invitation,' I'm getting into my stride now and my voice is stronger, sarcastic, my French gratifyingly fluent, 'but I don't think I want what you are offering. Affairs are just not my style.'

He drops his eyes, ashamed. And so he should be. Poor Marie-Louise. Poor Nathalie and Luc.

'I'm . . . I'm sorry, Gina,' he stammers. 'I didn't realise . . . I didn't think . . .'

'That I'd mind? Well, I do. You picked the wrong girl, I'm afraid. Sorry. Let's just not mention this again, okay?'

And I turn on my heel and stalk into the kitchen, firmly closing the door behind me.

Through the glass I see him climb into the cab of his truck, his shoulders sagging. He sits staring out through the windscreen for a few seconds before starting the engine and driving off. And I collapse into a chair and bury my fingers in my hair, clutching both sides of my head in anger. And not a little frustration. And, if I'm being perfectly honest, total disappointment and despair. If even Cédric, this quiet, strong, capable, warm, family-loving man, wants to have his cake and eat it too, what hope is there for womankind?

I groan, reliving the scene that has just taken place, cringing with embarrassment and humiliation. How awkward is it going to be when he comes back tomorrow? *If* he comes back tomorrow – maybe he won't now and my bedroom ceiling will remain forever unfinished and I'll have to lie in my lonely spinster bed every night and look up at it as a reminder of what could have been. Am I being a prude? Do other women merrily leap into bed with married men all the time at the drop of a hat? How awkward is it going to be when I run into Mireille? Or, oh God, Marie-Louise?

What a disaster. And I'm never going to meet anyone living here. But I can't go back to England yet. Unless I sell the house. That's what I'll have to do. Who in their right mind would want to live here anyway? With the distinctly unsettling history concerning my father and Liz? Where I've been coming all these years ignorant of that fact, thinking I loved this place, trusting my aunt, never imagining she was keeping a shadowy secret all along. Now the tears are rolling down my face, and I let them come, crying until I am emptied out. And afterwards, spent and exhausted, I go upstairs and lie down on the bed in the corner of the bedroom and gaze blankly up at the neatly patched ceiling until I fall asleep.

◆　◆　◆

I'm up early the next morning. I didn't sleep much anyway, inevitably. I'm determined to be brisk and businesslike when Cédric arrives. It's not going to take him long to finish up and I'm keen to get him out of both the house and my life as quickly as possible. I sit studiously at my computer, trying to convince myself – and anyone who should happen to come up the drive – that I'm terribly busy with some important research. The clock in the hall ticks ponderously and the minutes stretch to hours. No one appears. Well, what did I expect? He's obviously gone off in a huff, his male ego wounded by my rejection, and now the damn ceiling's never going to be finished.

It's early afternoon when I hear the sound of an engine in the courtyard. I glance towards the window and the wind is taken out of my sails somewhat when I see it's Pierre's motorbike that's arrived instead of Cédric's pickup. I go to the door.

'Hello,' I say politely.

Pierre is distant, preoccupied. 'Hello, Gina,' he says. 'I've come to finish things off. Sorry I couldn't get here this morning; Raphael needed me on another job. May I come in?' He shrugs a small rucksack off his shoulders.

'Of course.'

We both sound stilted and self-conscious. Clearly he knows what's happened and has come in his brother's place, to save him any further embarrassment. Well, at least Cédric must have a guilty conscience – that's something, I suppose.

Pierre busies himself upstairs, his silence a stark contrast to yesterday's cheerful banter. Apart from a somewhat stony request for water with which to mix the filler that he's going to skim over the joints, there's no conversation. I try to concentrate on my work, but the atmosphere is as oppressive as the build-up to a summer thunderstorm and my head feels hot and heavy. I push aside a pile of notebooks with a sigh. Honestly, why should I be made to feel like this? I'm the innocent one here. Who knows what Cédric has told his brother . . . Maybe he said I tried to make a pass at him. Ha! That really would be rich.

I make a mug of tea, not bothering to offer Pierre one as I can't face the cool rejection that I'm sure the offer will elicit. I take it outside to sit on the step in the late afternoon sunshine, to try and clear my head.

Eventually, Pierre comes down the stairs, packing tools and his rolled-up green overalls into his rucksack as he goes, evidently in a hurry to get out of my house and away as quickly as possible. I get up from the step, still clutching my mug.

'It's finished?' I ask.

'*Oui*,' he replies with a curt nod. He pulls on his leather jacket and shrugs the rucksack on to his back, then flings one leg over the motorbike. Just as he's about to fit the helmet over his unruly curls, he pauses and looks at me standing awkwardly by the step.

There's a pregnant silence. And then he speaks.

'It was an honest mistake,' he says. 'Cédric's really fallen for you. That's why he risked asking, in spite of what everyone has been saying about your situation. He thought it was just gossip.'

There's another silence as I try to digest what he's just said. Blimey, even his own brother is encouraging a little adultery on the side now.

And then I think, *you what?* Am I missing something in translation?

'Excuse me?' I say coolly. 'What's *my* situation got to do with it? It's his own situation that's the problem. I know you French are very broad-minded about these things but, bourgeois as it may seem, I'm not prepared to get involved with a married man.'

There's another silence as Pierre appears to be struggling to understand what I've just said.

'A married man,' he repeats stupidly.

Now he seems to be on the back foot, but I'm just starting to get into my stride. 'Yes. Poor Marie-Louise. I don't care how open a relationship they have, that's up to them – in fact, the whole situation is not something that interests me in the slightest.'

'Marie-Louise,' he repeats. Now he appears to be completely at a loss. Then he says, very calmly and reasonably, as you would to a lunatic whom you were trying not to derange any more than was clearly already the case, 'The same Marie-Louise who is married to Florian?'

'Precisely,' I say triumphantly.

And then I realise what he's just said. Now it's my turn to repeat his words. 'Marie-Louise is married to Florian.' I can feel the blood draining from my face.

Pierre looks at me curiously.

'But . . .' I stammer. 'But if Marie-Louise is married to Florian, who is married to Cédric?'

A grin begins to spread across Pierre's face as the *centime* begins to drop. And then his expression changes to one of sadness. 'Gina,' he says, speaking very slowly and clearly, as if to a complete idiot, 'Cédric's wife, Isabelle, died three years ago. Breast cancer. He hasn't looked at another woman since. Until you came along, that is. Marie-Louise was Isa's best friend from school days. She and Florian have been happily married for twelve years. They have three sons.' And then he says, more gently, 'How can you have lived here all these months and known nothing of this?'

How indeed? I hardly know myself. I suppose it's because I've been so immersed in trying to fathom my own family's complicated relationships that I've effectively shut myself away from the world.

'But she danced with him at Bastille Night,' I say lamely, struggling to make sense of everything I've just been told.

'That's because Florian has two left feet, and Cédric loves to dance,' says Pierre with a shrug.

'But Nathalie . . . and Luc . . .' I tail off lamely.

'Yeah, it's been tough for them, but Marie-Louise collects them from school some days, and others the school bus drops them at my mother's' – he nods in the direction of Mireille's house – 'so it's not a problem. That's what families are for, after all.'

There's another silence while I contemplate this, and then think of my own family, which seems far too sparse and somewhat lacking in comparison. And then, replaying the conversation we've just had, another thought occurs to me.

'Hang on a second,' I say indignantly. 'Just what are people saying about *my* situation?'

'We all knew you were with that terrible guy with the red face. Everyone saw you dancing with him at Bastille Night.'

'I was *never* with him,' I cry.

Pierre shrugs. 'That wasn't what it looked like to any of us. It really hurt Cédric's feelings seeing you together. And, heaven knows, he's had enough hurt to last a lifetime. We all told him to forget it, but he's much too pig-headed to listen to his own brothers, of course.'

I stand there, no doubt looking as much of an idiot as I feel. My anger fades, replaced by a sense of shame that I so misjudged Cédric. And then I realise that, despite my behaviour – my apparent coldness and the way I kept denying my feelings for him – Cédric still liked me enough to cling on to the hope that he might still be in with a chance. And he finally plucked up the courage to ask me out. I hear my shrill tirade from yesterday echoing in my head, berating him for being just another cheating bastard.

Pierre continues, with a nod at the mug in my hand, 'He even drank your horrible tea every day, just so he could have a chance to talk to you.'

'Oh, no, Pierre. I've made the most terrible mistake,' I wail.

But he's not really listening as he's taken out his mobile phone and is busy composing a text message. He obviously has more important things to deal with, like his own social life, for instance, than this crazy English woman who hasn't a clue what's going on in the world beyond her front gate.

With a final irritatingly dismissive shrug and a wave, he clamps the helmet firmly on his head and roars off down the drive and I'm left standing forlornly in the courtyard gazing after him.

Stunned, I sit down on the step, cradling my head in my hands as I try to absorb all I've just heard. How could I have been so wrong? I feel more of an outsider than ever, as I contemplate the intricate, tightly knit web of support that is the Thibault family. I've been living in a community that has observed and commented on my every move, while I've carried on blissfully unaware. I've been so wrapped up in my own affairs that I haven't made any attempt to find out more about my own neighbours, to understand them, to know their battles and their triumphs, to take part. And worst of all, I've now hurt and insulted one of the best men I've ever met, who has already suffered more than his share of loss and grief. I've blown my chances with what might just have been the man of my dreams.

A few minutes later, a car swishes by at the end of the drive and I glance up in time to catch a fleeting glimpse of a familiar dark-blue pickup. For a second my heart lurches as I think it's going to turn into the drive, but to my dismay it carries on along the lane. Cédric must be going to collect Nathalie and Luc from Mireille's.

I leap to my feet. I have to put this right. I'll go over and ask him to step outside so I can apologise, try to explain.

I hurry up the drive, anxious to get this over and done with, trying to think of the French for 'Sorry I'm such a complete bloody idiot' and 'Do you think you can ever find it in your heart to forgive me?' And then I see that a figure in dusty green overalls is coming towards me along the lane, hurrying just as much as I am.

As he draws near, I see the look on his face and I realise that, for once, Pierre's main priority wasn't sorting out his social life. He must have been texting his brother to let him know that the crazy English girl had got it all wrong. That she was so wrapped up in her own preoccupations she couldn't see what was going on right in front of her nose.

We stop, awkward now we're face to face again, and I begin to blurt out 'I'm so sorry . . .' when Cédric reaches out and puts a finger on my lips to stop me. His touch sends a jolt of longing through my body, so powerful that I lean into him and lose myself in his kiss.

The loneliness and frustration of the past months melt away as our bodies meld seamlessly together. The unspoken current of desire between us ignites into a blaze more powerful than any I've known before. And I know that all we can do is surrender ourselves to it. And then, over the sound of the pounding of my heart, I hear the hoarse, ratchet-like cry of a magpie, and another's triumphant answering call in the branches of the trees above our heads.

◆ ◆ ◆

Time passes – it could be five minutes, it could be fifty – and suddenly Cédric looks up, distracted by the sight of a small figure dancing along the lane towards us. I turn, still held in the circle of his strong arms, to see Nathalie. As she draws nearer, she calls, 'Papa, Mamie Mireille wants to know if you're going to ask Gina to come and have supper with us?'

Cédric looks down at me, his eyes tender, smiling, the threads of ancient pain and grief still just visible there, but overlain by so many other strands that make up his life, the fabric of which I'm only just starting to understand. 'It's not quite the romantic evening *à deux* that I had planned for our first date,' he laughs.

I stoop to hug Nathalie and brush back a strand of her dark hair from her eyes. Looking up at Cédric, I smile back. 'I can't think of anything more perfect,' I reply.

Nathalie takes hold of the hand that Cédric isn't holding and leads the two of us up the lane to the little house in the plum orchard.

Where Mireille, grinning broadly, already has an extra place set at the table.

Chapter 16

Our first proper date takes place the next evening. There's a concert at a local château and Cédric surprises me by suggesting we go. 'Ha!' he laughs. 'You didn't think a simple stonemason could be so cultured, did you, Gina? Well, to be honest, I really just want to get you to myself for once. My mother dotes on you and already regards you as a daughter, Nathalie adores you and even Luc says you're "cool", which is his highest accolade.'

I endure a lengthy session at the beauty salon, where the beautician purses her lips in disapproval at my lax English standards of personal care. She proceeds to wax, pluck and exfoliate me to within an inch of my life and I leave the salon feeling about half a stone lighter. Back home, I slip on my simple black dress, clasp a triple strand of pearls around my neck, and pin my hair back, with a tingling sense of anticipation.

It's a beautiful evening. The vines that surround the pretty château are turning golden in the light of early autumn. The concert is in a converted barn to one side of the main house and the music soars and floats in the peaceful space that rises into the rafters above us.

During the interval, Cédric introduces me to the château owners and one or two others who come up to say hello, but then, with a glint of determination in his eye, he steers me away. He picks up two glasses of chilled white wine from a table, saying, 'Come on, I'll show you some of my work.'

We wander into the gardens, down a path framed by tall cypress trees. There's a fountain at the far end, carved out of the local honey-coloured stone, and we make our way to it and perch on its rim. Its simple, clean lines are set off perfectly by a soft planting of silvery lavender and I brush my fingers over the dry purple spikes to release their fragrance.

'This is so beautiful,' I sigh, sipping my wine.

'Why, thank you, Mam'selle.'

'Carved by you? Well, you *are* a man of hidden talents! I thought you just fixed chimneys,' I tease.

'Ah, I assure you I do have one or two other talents that you have yet to discover.'

'Hmm, yes, like roofing. And of course ceilings . . .' And I peter out as he begins to kiss me, playfully at first, as if only to shut me up, but as I respond his kisses become deeper and more urgent.

'Let's go home,' I say huskily.

He takes my hand and leads me back up the path, our abandoned wine glasses glowing golden at the edge of the fountain in the last rays of the setting sun.

◆ ◆ ◆

We wake slowly the next morning, moving sleepily and languidly after the passionate haste of the night before.

I run my fingers over the lines of his face, gently tracing the faint fault lines of pain around his eyes that I'd noticed the very first time we met. I understand them a little better now.

As he holds me in his arms, I ask him about his wife, Isabelle, and her illness. It's still painful for him to talk about it and he seems touchingly vulnerable as he describes what he and the children went through as they watched her lose the struggle against her cancer, helpless in the face of its terrible destructive force. 'I've tried to protect Luc and Nathalie as much as possible. That's been my main priority ever since we lost Isa.' His voice cracks as he relives the loss. 'And of course my family have been wonderful, supporting the children and me.'

'What a good thing you're all so close. I know it can never replace the children's mother, but a loving extended family like yours is a wonderful thing, I can see.' I can't help contrasting it with my own family, which seems so lacking in comparison.

Cédric smiles at me. 'Why such a sad expression, my lovely Gina?' He kisses my forehead gently, and the slight frown that had been gathering there melts away.

I pull away a little, turning so that I can face him. I'm hesitant, unsure whether to confide in him. After the series of betrayals by everyone I thought I was closest to that I've experienced in the past year, learning to trust anyone ever again has felt like an impossible struggle. But looking into his face now, I begin to let my guard down, reassured by the look I see written in his eyes. There's a solidity about him, not just in the strong lines of his muscular body but in the way he seems so rooted into this land, so comfortable in his life here, so sure of his priorities when it comes to his family.

I tell him about finding the photo, my worst fears and suspicions, my feelings of devastation, complicated by the sense of frustration at having nobody I can ask to find out the truth of the matter. Despite my tentative questioning of Hugh and Celia Everett, no one seems to have any certain knowledge of whether or not my father visited Liz here after that first encounter when the picture must have been taken. The only person who might be able to tell me is the one I can never ask: my own mother.

Cédric whistles through his teeth in disbelief at the revelations, then lies silent for a while, digesting what I've told him. Finally, he shakes his head. 'You could ask my mother, I suppose. Mireille didn't know Liz for very long, but they did become very close friends. Maybe your aunt confided in her before she died?' He hesitates. 'Or maybe you just have to try and accept that this is something you'll probably never know.' He holds up a hand as I start to protest. 'I know it's hard. But you have to try to respect their wish to keep it a secret in order to protect your mother. Imagine the devastation – her husband and her own sister. The important thing for you now is to move on and learn to trust again.' Then, with a slow smile, he adds, 'And I think I know just the man for that job.'

'Oh yes? Well, perhaps you could give me his number then,' I reply airily, laughing as he pulls me to him and leaves me in no doubt at all as to exactly who that man is.

◆　◆　◆

Life falls into a new routine. While Cédric is at work with his brothers, I push on with my Master of Wine studies, making good progress now that I have a structure to my weeks and a local support network of experts to call on when I need help. In the evenings I go to Cédric's, or he and the children come to me, and we have supper together. By unspoken agreement, I never sleep over at his house and we stay apart on nights when the children will be at school the next day. It's new to me, having to accommodate family life, and I begin to want more, especially as I grow to love Luc and Nathalie in a way that surprises me. But I sense Cédric is holding back a little, still feeling the need to protect his children, and a tiny niggle of insecurity stirs in me now and then, a voice of doubt that whispers, *He loved Isabelle more than he loves me.*

The weekends are easier, a whirlwind of noise and fun and busyness, spent watching Luc's football matches and Nathalie's ballet classes, and getting together with the ever-changing kaleidoscope that is Cédric's family – his brothers and their wives, uncles, aunts, Mireille of course, and the children's myriad cousins. And that's before we even get started on the friends. When I express my bewilderment at this sprawling community that seems to have swallowed me up, Cédric laughs. 'Yes, around here everybody knows everyone else. We all went to school together. Our parents all went to school together. Our children all go to school together. And so it goes on.'

And when the little pang of insecurity inside me raises its head and whispers, *And I'll always be an outsider here*, I push it firmly to one side.

We get together for the usual family gathering at Mireille's house for Sunday lunch and, once everyone has gone, Nathalie and Luc settle down to watch a DVD and Cédric goes outside to fix a loose section of guttering. Mireille looks after him fondly as we dry the last few pots and pans. 'My helpful son. That's how he shows his love, you know – fixing things. Which made it all the harder for him when Isa fell ill. Something that couldn't be fixed.' She pauses, reflecting. 'That's how I knew he'd fallen for you, after not looking at another woman for so long, when he was so keen to fix your roof. That and the fact that he was even prepared to drink tea and eat those – *comment ça se dit?* – HobNobs to find an excuse to spend time with you.'

We work in companionable silence for a few moments, each deep in our own thoughts. And then I think, it's now or never.

I take a breath.

'Mireille, did Liz ever confide in you about my father? You see, I know something happened between them, long ago, before I was even born . . .' And I explain about discovering the photo and the missing negatives.

She's silent for a while, giving nothing away. Finally, she hugs me, then holds me at arm's length so she can look into my eyes.

'Ah, Gina, I can see this has been so hard for you, discovering that the past is perhaps not what you thought it was. But whatever may or may not have happened between them is ancient history now. And so you have to wonder whether it's really all that important to know exactly what went on when, and for how long. What good would that do you? It might just make you suffer more. It could even drive more of a wedge between you and your mother. Being the one left behind isn't easy either, you know – just ask Cédric. And your mother needs you, no matter how strong and independent she may seem.'

She smooths my hair back from my face, a gesture of tenderness and love. 'As I see it, and I know it's not easy, the most important thing is for you to forgive and to move on. Don't let what you don't know eat away at you. Life's too short for that. Being able to let go is as important as it is difficult to do. So my advice to you is to let this whole affair rest now. Try to get on with your life, and try to remember them both with love. After all, the one thing you do know is that they both loved you very, very much indeed. And I've seen enough of life and death to know that, in the end, love is all that we have.'

She pats my hand reassuringly and I nod slowly.

'I know you're right, Mireille. You're so wise. I'll try my best.'

'And you have people here who love you too, you know. You're becoming more and more important to Cédric and the children. I haven't seen my son so happy since before Isa became ill. And for that I thank you with all my heart.'

She hugs me again. 'Now, let's go and see if we can prise Luc and Nathalie away from the TV for a game of cards.'

As we're leaving that evening, Cédric says to Mireille, 'Are you okay to have the children after school every afternoon this week? We're starting the new job on the *mairie* in Sainte-Foy. All the upper stonework and part of the roof. We want to get on with it before the weather changes, so I may need to work late.'

Mireille reaches for her diary. 'I can do everything except Wednesday. I've got a hair appointment that afternoon.'

'I could have them on Wednesday,' I offer eagerly. 'I can come and wait at Mireille's gate for the school bus if you like, then take them back to my house.'

Mireille nods approvingly. But Cédric says casually, 'Oh no, don't worry, Gina. Marie-Louise will pick them up – she'll be at the school to collect Hugo anyway. And I'm sure you'll be busy getting on with your work.'

'Okay, fine, if that's easiest then,' I reply lightly. But I feel cut to the core that he seems not to trust me with his children. I try not to mind, but in truth I do and it's driving a wedge between us. I think Mireille's noticed because she pats my arm in a conciliatory manner as she says goodbye.

I hug Luc and Nathalie and kiss Cédric, then make my lonely way back along the lane as they head home for their Sunday evening, *en famille*.

◆ ◆ ◆

Annie's call is a welcome distraction from the particularly heavy assignment that I'm working on for the Master of Wine course. She's as bubbly and irrepressible as ever. And when I confess how mistaken I'd been about Cédric, she crows with glee.

'I knew it! You're as readable as a copy of *Hello!* magazine, Gina Peplow. I told you there was something major going on between you and him the very first time I saw you together. Well, well, well, you *are* getting in deep. I suppose now I won't be able to persuade you to come over for a girls' weekend and some serious retail therapy, which was why I'm calling.'

When our conversation is over, I put down the phone with a sigh and look out of the window at the cold grey mist that's swathing the bare trees. Autumn's well and truly arrived and there's a damp chill in the air. Lafite and I are snug in the kitchen with the fire burning cheerily. I throw on another log, sending a flurry of sparks up the chimney.

To tell the truth, the thought of a trip to the bright lights and sumptuous shopfronts of London sounds pretty appealing right now. And Cédric's working all hours on the job at the *mairie* so I've hardly seen him apart from at weekends, and then we're surrounded by family and friends as usual so we scarcely have any time alone together.

'He probably wouldn't miss me if I did go,' I grumble to Lafite, who twitches his ears as if trying to flick away my tetchy words.

The phone rings again and as I answer it I notice it's a UK number. 'Yes?' I say, expecting it to be Annie calling back with some last snippet of important gossip that she'd forgotten to impart.

'Gina, it's Harry. Harry Wainright.'

'Harry! What a lovely surprise. Sorry, I thought you were going to be Annie McKenzie. I've just finished talking to her. How are you? Enjoying retirement, I hope.'

'Ah yes, all's well here. And Annie seems to be thriving. I spoke to her just now to get your number. How's the MW course going?'

'Well, no one said it was going to be easy, but I'm enjoying it. Doing okay so far, I think.'

'Now, Gina, your ears must have been burning yesterday. I had lunch with Charles Barrow – remember him? MD of Barrow Brothers?'

Of course I remember him. He's a well-known figure in the wine world in England and Barrow Brothers is one of the most prestigious wine and spirits companies there is.

'He was asking me whether I know of any France specialists. They've got an opening and are looking for someone with exactly your background and expertise. Anyway, the long and the short of it is that he wants to interview you and I think you're in with the best possible chance. The fact that you're doing your MW qualification too makes you an even stronger candidate.'

I can hardly breathe, I'm so excited. This is everything I've ever dreamed of career-wise. Harry gives me Charles Barrow's contact details and I stammer my thanks, scarcely able to take it all in.

I put the phone down again and then freeze. What am I thinking? How can I make this work? I can't imagine life without Cédric and the children. At the thought of losing them, I feel a pang of pain so strong it takes my breath away.

It's the most amazing opportunity. And the timing couldn't be any worse.

◆ ◆ ◆

I decide to say nothing to Cédric until I've spoken to Charles Barrow. After all, there's no point in saying anything at all if it turns out he's not seriously interested. But after a lengthy phone interview, it seems the job's mine if I want it.

I feel sick. Sick with excitement on the one hand, and sick with anxiety and doubt on the other. There's a heaviness in my heart that surprises me. This is the career opportunity I always thought I'd wanted. If I was still living in England, it would be easy. I'd jump at the chance, secure in the knowledge that I was taking the safe route again. I should be over the moon. But my heart is heavy at the thought of losing Cédric. Of not seeing Nathalie and Luc, not sharing their lives as they grow up. Of not being a part of something that's so much more than I've ever known before – something worth caring about. It's not an easy choice, but I know I couldn't bear to lose them.

Cédric and I have arranged to have dinner together tonight and we've got some serious talking to do.

I've cooked *boeuf bourguignon*, enriched with a generous slosh of red wine and simmered for hours until the house is filled with the delicious smell of the herb-infused juices, which only makes my stomach churn all the more. I set the table for two, folding napkins and lighting candles. I turn the lights down low to create a romantic atmosphere, although in part it's to hide how nervous I feel. I pour myself a glass of wine, trying to steady my nerves. If he really loves me, he'll be glad for me, I tell myself. Perhaps we can find a way to make it work. How, I'm not sure. There's no way he and the children could uproot themselves from here to move to London. And I know I won't have many weekends free as the job will involve attending tastings and shows at frequent intervals.

Cédric arrives, and my heart somersaults at the sight of him, freshly showered after his day's work, wearing a clean shirt and faded jeans and carrying a bunch of fragrant white roses. We kiss, and I hold him tightly, pressing my body against his and melting into him. Every nerve ending in me tingles with the knowledge that this is right, that we're meant to be together.

Cédric chats away over dinner, filling me in on the latest gossip from Sainte-Foy. The *mairie* is the hub of the town, dominating the central square, and working on the roof there, he's in a position to watch all the comings and goings of daily life. I listen in silence as he describes the absurd dramas of the community with fond humour, his face animated, his handsome features relaxed. He's mopping up the last traces of gravy from his plate when he suddenly looks up at me and says, 'Why so quiet tonight, Gina? There's something on your mind.'

And so I tell him. I explain about Harry's call and the interview and everything Charles Barrow's told me about the job. He sits quietly, letting me speak, hearing me out. And when I finish, he looks down at his empty plate, very carefully sets his knife and fork on it and, still not looking at me, says, 'I see.'

There's a silence that's loud with pain and disappointment and I rush to fill it.

'Of course, I haven't had all the details of the job offer yet, and nothing's been decided.'

'But there is a job offer,' he says quietly. He raises his eyes to meet my beseeching ones, the fault lines of pain fracturing across his face. 'I understand, of course I do. I know how much this must mean to you.' He pauses, swallowing hard as if his throat is obstructed by a big lump of anguish. 'It's just . . . I love you so much, Gina. *We* love you so much. All of us – Luc and Nathalie, my whole family. I can't bear to see them hurt all over again.'

He stops and shakes his head. 'Now I feel I shouldn't have let myself trust you.'

The niggling little voice of insecurity and uncertainty deep inside me whispers, *I don't belong here; he doesn't really trust me; in the end you can't trust anyone.*

And my own anguish suddenly overwhelms everything. 'You never trusted me though, did you, Cédric?' I blurt out. 'You didn't trust me enough to let me pick up the children. You never really let me be properly part of your family. I could never match up to

185

Isabelle, could I?' I regret the words as soon as they're out of my mouth, but it's too late to take them back. They hang in the air between us, filling the room with their brutal finality.

And that's when it strikes me that we're both talking in the past tense. As you do when you know something is over.

'And you know what?' I finish with a sense of bitter despair that almost makes me choke. 'In my experience, even family can betray you. So in the end maybe it's better if I stand on my own two feet.'

Chapter 17

The really sad thing is, I realise in the days that follow, that the hurt and pain we'd both suffered in our past relationships spilled over into this one. Once bitten, twice shy, as the saying goes. That damage went deeper than I'd thought it did. If neither one of us is able to trust the other, how could we ever have a future together?

Just as well we found that out sooner rather than later, I tell myself as I start to pack up the house. There's a lot to do to get it ready for selling. There's no point dragging things out here, where I'll bump into Cédric or Mireille or any one of a hundred members of the Thibault clan if I so much as venture out of my front gate.

The offer letter from Barrow Brothers has arrived. It's everything I could have asked for. Slightly more, in fact, when it comes to the salary.

So why do I feel so empty inside?

Mum's flying out to help me finish packing up and to share the driving home. I've hired a 'man with a van' to bring back the few things I want and I'm leaving the rest here to be sold with the house.

Lafite will have to suffer the indignity of being micro-chipped and having his vaccinations topped up so that he can be issued with his pet passport. He glares at me balefully as I stash Liz's files of negatives and photographs into cardboard boxes, as if he knows he's not going to like the next stage of his life, incarcerated in a London flat. My pride won't let me ask Mireille to keep him.

I hesitate when I get to the sitting room. The urn with Liz's ashes is still there on the coffee table. Maybe I'll scatter them among the vines just before I go, I think. It might not be entirely legal, but Liz would have got a kick out of helping nourish future vintages. Perhaps Mum would like to be there for that. I close the door softly behind me. I move carefully these days, feeling as if any sudden movement might make me shatter into a thousand pieces. I drift from room to room like a ghost, numb with grief and a sense of loss even more overwhelming than that which has gone before . . .

◆ ◆ ◆

Having my mother here helps a little. She busies herself with lending a hand to pack up the house and we work in silence alongside one another. I know she must be worried about me because she so readily agreed to come when I asked her. I realise it's the first time she's ever stayed in this house.

It's a grey, blustery day, the autumn wind whipping angrily through the bare branches of the trees. We're wrapping china in sheets of newspaper, our fingers grimy with smudged black ink.

'Your father would have approved thoroughly of your job, you know, and been so proud of how well you're doing with the Master of Wine qualification,' she tells me, breaking the silence, trying to raise my spirits. I know I'm terrible company at the moment.

I nod. 'Well, I've still got to get through the exams in the summer, and then write my dissertation next year. But it's good to have that to focus on. I'm going to be really busy getting stuck into the job too. And I thought I might try writing a couple of pieces and submitting them to the wine magazines. You never know; maybe I'll end up following in Dad's footsteps after all.'

There's another pause, as I wonder whether I can ask the next question I want to put to my mother. I swallow nervously and then say as nonchalantly as possible, 'Did Dad used to come and stay here? When he was over on his wine-tasting trips, I mean.'

Mum considers my question for a moment, apparently concentrating hard on folding paper around a teacup. Then she lifts her head and gives me a searching look, still saying nothing. The silence begins to grow heavy with unspoken meaning and I drop my eyes. I pick up a sugar bowl and fiddle nervously with the lid.

Finally, she speaks.

'He loved her, you know,' she says very quietly. 'I did wonder whether you had realised.'

There's another pause and I say nothing, my heart beating hard as I digest what she's just said.

She gazes, unseeing, at the wrapped cup in her hands and then slowly places it in the cardboard box that sits on the table between us. She moves to the window, looking out at the garden where a pair of magpies pick their way across the lawn before fluttering off into the branches of the cedar tree.

'David and Liz met here in France. It was a couple of years before I knew him. They fell deeply in love. But her career in the States was just taking off and his was firmly based in England. She shut up the house here and took off on her travels. A long-distance relationship would have been impossible, and they both knew it. She was always a strong woman, my sister. She realised what she was giving up, she once told me, but she also knew that she had to put her career first. In those days it was an either/or decision. She knew her work was the only way she could be true to herself.'

Mum turns away from the window and smiles. 'You meant the world to her, Gina. You really were the daughter she never had. She was so proud of you. I kept out of the way when you came here for your summer holidays – I wanted to give her that time with you, as a gift. I was grateful to her, you see, for the decision she made. Ultimately, it gave me the two most important things in my life: David and you.'

'When did you and Dad meet, then?' I ask.

'More than a year after she left. There was an exhibition of photographs at a gallery in London and a couple of Liz's pictures were included. We met at the private view, standing in front of a photo of Andy Warhol that she'd taken in his studio. So, in a funny way, she brought us together. We didn't know that when we met – we only pieced it together afterwards.'

'How did you feel, though, about them having been in love?'

'I came to see it was just a part of our shared history. I never doubted them. I knew neither of them would betray my trust. They each cared for me so much. We were all able to move on.' She reaches across to me. 'It's really important that you know this, Gina – that he never regretted the decision he'd made. He always said it was the best thing ever, being a father to you. And a good husband to me.' She gives me a rueful glance. 'I may not be the most demonstrative person on the planet, but David always knew how much he was loved.'

She reaches over to hug me. I hug her back, hard. I see it all so differently now that I understand.

There are a thousand more questions I want to ask, but I sense that now is not the time. Mum's already given me an awful lot to digest. And anyway, perhaps, as Mireille said, sometimes it's better just to let the past be.

Then she continues, in a brisker tone, 'Now that we've got all that out in the open, there's something else I wanted to ask you about. Liz's ashes. Have you already scattered them somewhere?'

I shake my head. 'No. I wasn't sure what to do with them. And I don't really know what's allowed under French law. They're in the sitting room.'

'Well, I don't know what you think about this idea, but I wonder whether it's time now to let them be together. Why don't we scatter them where we did Dad's, beside his bench at the edge of the ridge?'

I look carefully into her face, but her expression is calm, happier and more peaceful than I've seen it in years. 'Would you really be okay with that?' I ask.

'The way I see it, they couldn't be together in life, so it's right that they should finally be together in death. I still loved both of them very much, you know. Families are complicated things, Gina. I quite like the thought of having the pair of them at the bottom of the garden.' Mum strokes my hair. 'Anyway, they'd both have been so proud of you now.'

I'm silent for a few moments, still trying to absorb everything she's just told me. And then I sit bolt upright, realisation dawning. I don't have to do what Liz did. It's not an either/or decision any more.

Suddenly I see it all so clearly. I have a choice. Staying here may not be the safe route. There'll be challenges along the way. But perhaps I'm not meant to take the safe route. Perhaps I'm meant to carve out my own path. And I think that maybe, with Cédric walking beside me, I'll be able to do it. He and I will help one another to heal those old wounds. We won't let the pain from the past stop us from finding joy in the present. Together, we'll learn how to trust again, with our hearts wide open.

I know that my own heart is here to stay. And that will be enough to make it work.

In shock, I face my mother, aghast. 'Oh, Mum, I think I've made the most terrible mistake.'

She smiles at me serenely. 'Gina, my darling, there are very many ways to have a successful career. And you're only going to find the love of your life once, you know. My advice to you is to grab hold of your new life here with both hands and hang on tight!'

I dial Cédric's mobile with shaking hands, knowing that I have to speak to him straight away. I need to put right all that's got lost in translation between us. To tell him that I know we can both learn to trust one another after all, that we can find a way to build our own lives together.

There's no reply and Cédric's phone cuts over to voicemail.

I snatch up my car keys and head out of the kitchen door.

'Drive safely!' Mum calls after me.

The Thibault brothers' lorry is parked in front of the *mairie* and I pull up beside it with a jerk. Raphael, who's unloading roof tiles from the back, looks startled to see me arrive so precipitously out of the blue, but pulls himself together and comes to open my car door.

'Where's Cédric? I need to talk to him. Straight away,' I gasp. I can't let another minute go by without knowing that it's not too late.

Raphael gestures upwards, where the front of the building is swathed in scaffolding. Florian comes over to see what's going on. When he catches sight of me he calls up to Pierre, who's halfway up a ladder, a stack of tiles balanced on his shoulder. Pierre peers down and then calls up to Cédric, who appears from behind the balustrade that runs around the edge of the roof. 'What is it?' he shouts.

'There's someone here who wants to talk to you,' bellows Florian, pointing towards me. His words are snatched away by a gust of wind.

'I can't hear you,' Cédric shouts back.

'Gina's here!' yells Pierre, pointing down at me.

Cédric peers over the edge of the stonework and takes in the scene below him in the square. 'What do you want? Are you all right, Gina?'

The fact that he's concerned about me, even a tiny bit, gives me a surge of hope and I shout up to him, 'I've made a mistake.' But my lips are dry and my voice comes out in a squeak.

Cédric holds a hand to his ear, gesturing that he can't hear.

'She says she's made a mistake,' bellows Raphael.

Pierre relays the message upwards, in case his brother still hasn't got the gist of it. 'She's made a mistake. Again!'

I bridle slightly at the 'again'. But actually perhaps he has a point, so I let it go.

By now, several passers-by have stopped to watch, craning their heads to look up at Cédric high above us all. He hesitates, unsure, reluctant to climb down.

I shout again, louder now, so that he'll hear me over the blustering wind. 'I love you. I'm not leaving. I want to stay here with you and Luc and Nathalie.'

A couple of shopkeepers have now come to stand in their doorways, the better to enjoy the scene that's unfolding in the *place*, a welcome diversion on a quiet morning. A van pulls up, the driver rolling down his window and craning his head to see what everyone's looking at. A car comes up behind him and toots impatiently, but the van driver is now deep in conversation with one of the shopkeepers, who's filling him in on what he's missed, gesturing towards me and then to Cédric up on the roof, and so the driver of the car rolls down her window too for a better look, oblivious to the traffic jam that's starting to build up behind her.

Two *gendarmes* appear out of the *mairie* and I think maybe they're going to arrest me for public disorder. I need to get my message across – and fast. I throw back my head, take a deep breath, searching for the exact phrase I need.

'*J'ai envie de toi!*' I shout against the wind, with every ounce of strength in my body. I want you. I need you. I desire you. And the whole of the town now knows it.

The brothers cheer, and the assembled crowd – including the *gendarmes* – applauds as Cédric scrambles down the ladder, jumping the last few feet.

He pauses in front of me, still a little wary. 'Are you sure you know what you're saying?' he asks, his voice trembling, his eyes so full of hope that my heart lurches with relief.

And I whisper, 'I know exactly what I'm saying. I love you. And now I understand that that's all that matters.'

'But your work . . .'

'I'll find something here. After all, we are in the middle of the world's biggest and best-known wine region. There must be something I can do.'

I put my arms out and he hugs me to him, holding me so tightly that I know this time he'll never let me go.

Epilogue...

It's an early summer's night and the moonlight is streaming in through the skylights in the bedroom ceiling. I rub my eyes, which are gritty with tiredness, and glance over at the clock. Two twenty. It must be a good two years now since my insomnia began and I've given up all hope of ever having a full night's sleep again.

I wonder briefly where my notebook has got to. Not that I need it any more – finding the time to write a to-do list these days is about as unlikely as finding an affordable bottle of Château Pétrus. I haven't seen it for ages, but it's probably buried under a pile of papers in the study. Or maybe Nathalie has been using it to play 'Businesswomen' with her friends again, clicking about in a pair of my high heels and one of my old work jackets as she dreams of her own future.

I gaze at my husband, who is fast asleep beside me, worn out at the end of another hard day's work. Downstairs, Luc and Nathalie are asleep in their rooms. Luc will have his beloved phone plugged into his ears, having fallen asleep listening to his latest playlist. He's taken it upon himself to try to educate me, introducing me to more up-to-date artists, although we still dance around the kitchen to some of my old music when no one's looking.

And I know Lafite will be curled up at the end of Nathalie's bed, watching over her from his favourite spot.

In my arms, our newborn baby son is just dropping off again after his 2 a.m. feed. Cédric says he's going to grow up to be a famous wine writer, like his English grandfather and his mother. (In my case, I'm not sure that the one article to date published in *Carafe* magazine qualifies me for fame, although Mireille still carries a copy around in her handbag and has shown it to everyone from the postman to the mayor. But then I do have to fit in my writing between looking after my children and selling the wines of a number of local producers into the UK, so at least it's a start.)

But *I* hope our son is going to follow in the footsteps of his father and his namesake uncle and be the next stonemason called Pierre. Forming the next band of Thibault Frères, perhaps, along with his brother Luc and some of his cousins.

I ease myself carefully out of bed, still cradling little Pierre in my arms, and gently put him back in his cot. His long dark eyelashes flutter on his cheeks but he doesn't wake.

As I stand gazing down at him in the moonlight, I think about families, picturing the serried ranks of photographs in their frames on the dresser in the kitchen. There's a cluster of photos of Luc and Nathalie; there's a beautiful print of Isabelle hugging her two beloved children, her face glowing before her cruel illness took hold; there's a picture of Cédric and me emerging from the little chapel at Saint André on our wedding day last year, in which I'm wearing Liz's vintage top over a flowing skirt of cream silk, my mother's pearl-and-diamond choker, which she'd worn on her own wedding day, around my neck; and there's a large print, taken by Robert Cortini from the catwalk above the wine vats in the *chai* at Château de la Chapelle, of a long table bedecked with wisteria and white lilac, at which a hundred people are raising their glasses to the bride and groom. I know that *chai* so well now that I'm part of the team, selling their wines as well as handling the marketing for a group of local châteaux that I've persuaded to band together.

And tucked at the back are three black-and-white photos: one of Liz, one of my mother and one of Dad. Of course it's not *the* photo of my father. That ended up as a few extra ashes among the ones Mum and I scattered, where the garden gives on to the view of the Downs, one breezy June day last year.

Only now that I have children of my own do I fully appreciate how much these three loved me. More than love itself.

I think of Mum, alone in her house, keeping herself busy with her bridge and her shopping, the only men in her life these days her good friends Peter Jones and Harvey Nichols . . . An idea occurs to me.

As I ease myself back into bed, Cédric turns over with a sigh and puts out an arm to pull me to him. 'Are you awake?' I whisper.

'Hmm,' he mumbles drowsily.

'Does Patrick Cortini play bridge?' I whisper again.

Cédric opens one eye and smiles at me. 'Ah, Gina,' he whispers back, 'I love the crazy things you say.' And he falls straight back into a deep sleep once more.

Never mind, I'll ask Marie-Louise and Christine when I see them at the school gates tomorrow; they're sure to know.

I turn over and pull up the duvet. The clock says 2.35 a.m.

Suddenly, the moonlit room is flooded with fluting, liquid birdsong. A nightingale is singing in the oak trees outside.

I hear my father's voice saying to me, 'They are the only bird to sing through the night, Gina. And they only sing while their babies are in the nest. Once they fledge, the parent is silent again. But it's as if, while their children are with them, they can't help but express the joy in their overflowing hearts.'

Smiling to myself, I close my eyes. And think, *I know just how they feel.*

ACKNOWLEDGEMENTS

Thank you to all the people who helped me with the writing of this book, one of the trio in the *Escape to France* series. It was first published as *The French for Love*. But this edition, renamed *Light Through the Vines*, is published by the Lake Union team at Amazon Publishing and I am most grateful for their encouragement and input, as well as for the opportunity to revise some sections of the original manuscript and bring it up to date.

Huge thanks, as always, to my wonderful editorial team: Victoria Oundjian, Sammia Hamer, Mike Jones, Jenni Davis and Swati Gamble. And to my fabulous agent, Madeleine Milburn, as well as Liv Maidment and the rest of the team at the Madeleine Milburn Agency, for all their help and support.

I lived in France for seven years and it was there that I found the inspiration to write this novel. Of course, all the characters are entirely fictional, but the Thibault brothers' very high standards of expertise and craftsmanship were inspired by the Feltrin brothers and their team, who worked miracles to help us create a dream home in France. (And there really is a stonemason called Pierre.)

I am very grateful to those brave souls in the winemaking world who let me loose on their vines and in their cellars: Eric Bonneville and his team at Château L'Enclos, Jacqui and Jean-Michel de Robillard, and especially Pierre Charlot, whose Château des Chapelains in St André-et-Appelles became the inspiration for so much in this book.

Thanks to all at the Confrérie des Vins de Sainte-Foy Bordeaux, who honoured me by awarding me the title of Chevalier of the appellation, and to Florent Niautou in the oenology lab at St André-et-Appelles for sharing his passion for winemaking.

And finally, my love and thanks go to my family and friends. We've come a long way, through some dark and difficult times, but there has always been light through the vines.

READ ON FOR AN EXTRACT
FROM FIONA VALPY'S
THE SEASON OF DREAMS

Once upon a time, not so very long ago, nor so very far away, an ancient château sat on a hilltop among the vines, high above a golden river.

Halfway through their first season at Château Bellevue de Coulliac, Sara felt she was beginning to get into the swing of the new business. She enjoyed being part of the magic and helping make each dream wedding come to pass in their stone castle perched above the deep valley of the Dordogne.

It was supposed to be picture-perfect, her new life out here in France with Gavin, beginning to build their future, following dreams of their own . . .

So why, in these quieter moments, did she feel such a growing sense of suffocation?

It was a hot summer's night and with a sigh of relief she sank on to the bed and slid her aching legs across the cool sheets. Her nerves were still jangling from the way Gavin had put her down – again – that evening. It seemed to be happening more and more often and she regularly found herself biting her lip, swallowing the words that rose in her throat so that they accumulated in her chest in a big, hard, unspoken lump.

It had been just one more small dig when she was running through the arrangements for the wedding with the caterers. A snide remark about her being such a control freak, that at every celebration there was someone who knew how to put the 'un' in 'fun' and that person was usually Sara. It had hurt and he knew it. Somehow, he always managed to make her out to be the boringly responsible one, while he was the life and soul of the party.

She had tried to talk to him about it in private on previous occasions when he'd made her feel small in front of others. But he'd swept her concerns aside, telling her not to be so petty – that it was just part of the double act they put on for their clients; she should man up and learn to take a joke.

The strain of restoring an ancient French home and building a business had taken a toll on both of them. They'd planned for the renovations, of course – the new roof on the barn, the need to completely rewire the place, the gallons of plaster and paint, and hours of hard work. But they hadn't fully grasped what a bottomless money pit the restoration of a historic building can be, especially in a foreign country where the planning regulations and restrictions were tortuous to say the least. It had been a stressful time, although the sense of achievement still made it all worthwhile.

And, through it all, there had been nothing more guaranteed to focus the mind entirely than the immovable, terrifying, brick-wall deadline of the first wedding of the season looming ahead of them in the diary. It would have been completely terrifying were it not for the fact that she and Gavin were in it together, supporting and encouraging one another through the occasional dispiriting days of that first cold, damp winter with builders' dust clogging every pore of their bodies and their hands blistered and scarred with unaccustomed labouring.

But as she reminded herself of this, unconsciously Sara raised a hand to her throat, as if to soothe the feeling of choked panic that seemed now to have lodged itself there.

It wasn't just the stifling heat and the relentless cycle of arrivals, weddings, departures and then, immediately, preparations for the next event. When she stopped to think, she had a horrible niggling feeling that she'd made a huge mistake. Perhaps the biggest mistake of her life, so far at least. For Sara had burned all her bridges coming out here, selling her tiny London flat and saying goodbye to her burgeoning landscape gardening business, setting her sights firmly on the seductive promise of a sunny future in France, married life with Gavin, a home, a family . . .

She'd taken a chance – a leap into the unknown – when Gavin got down on one knee and proposed not just marriage but a move to France too, and now it was making her feel increasingly uneasy. He'd changed a lot over the past two years.

It was only once the first wedding season had started that she'd noticed that Gavin seemed to need to bolster his own ego by finding fault with her in hundreds of little ways, criticising her efforts and undoing her decisions. Subtly and inexorably, she'd felt her sense of self being eroded. Gavin seemed to have taken over, their partnership morphing into a dictatorship as he began making unilateral decisions, disregarding her suggestions, overriding her plans.

Of course, she told herself, if she was being completely honest it was partly her fault too, for giving in. It felt like when she talked, no one listened. So it had become easier just to do things Gavin's way in the château and instead to channel her own creative energy into the garden, studiously avoiding confronting the sneaking suspicion that the foundations of their relationship were anything less than solid.

Perhaps it was just as well she was kept so busy most of the time, keeping these panicked thoughts firmly at bay. She needed to reserve her energy for the guests, making sure each wedding was perfect.

Every event had its own very particular character, a projection of the personalities of each unique set of participants, and she really did enjoy seeing how each couple stamped their own mark on the proceedings, making their own private fairy tale come true.

Today's wedding had been particularly hard work. The mother of the bride, Mrs Nolan, had been a Fusser, incapable of leaving Sara and Gavin to get on with their side of things, popping up at Sara's elbow at frequent intervals to add some more requests to the already lengthy list of her daughter's special requirements.

'Ever so sorry, but have you got some pink ribbon? Only Brittany wants Melanie to have Bitsy accompany her up the aisle and we've only got the yellow lead with us. And yellow will clash with the bridesmaids' dresses. No, not that pale pink, more of a cerise . . . Oh, well, if that's all you've got, we'll just have to make do. Brittany's not going to like it though.' Eventually, Sara had managed to unearth a length of bright pink ribbon from a drawerful of wrapping paper and Brittany's own personal sun had re-emerged from behind that particular black cloud.

There had been a nerve-wracking moment in the chapel when Melanie, the maid of honour, had lost her grip on the length of pink ribbon tied to the diamante collar of Brittany's handbag-sized chihuahua, Bitsy, and the little dog had made a run for it, almost making it out of the door. Luckily, Gavin's fast reflexes had saved the day and, muttering 'Never work with children or animals . . .', he'd returned Bitsy to the waiting arms and abundantly displayed cleavage of Melanie.

Mrs Nolan was not just a Fusser, she was also a Talker. Sara's ears still rang with the stream-of-consciousness chatter that had accompanied her for much of the day. 'Of course, we wanted Colchester, but Brittany said, "No, Mum, this is my big day, it's got to be somewhere really classy." And with a name like hers, France it had to be. We named her after the place she was conceived, you see.'

'How nice,' Sara responded politely, only half listening as she stacked plates into the dishwasher. 'So you named her after the region.'

Mrs Nolan had looked at her blankly.

'No, love – the ferries. First night of our honeymoon, the crossing from Portsmouth to Santander and then we drove down to the Costa Blanca for a fortnight. Not so many cheap flights in those days, and of course it was before Derek's business had taken off, so there was no spare cash back then. Our little princess doesn't know how lucky she is, off to Bangkok and God knows where for *her* honeymoon.'

We'd better hope her first child isn't conceived on the first night too then, thought Sara, going out to meet the florist and oversee the flower arrangements in the chapel as per Mrs Nolan's detailed instructions.

Mr Nolan, in contrast to his garrulous wife, was a man of few words. He'd made a fortune in the trucking industry, which his wife and daughter were now doing their best to spend. He'd passed the morning sitting in a deckchair in the shade of a cedar tree, with the desperate air of a man who'd been sentenced to deliver a wedding speech for his daughter when he'd really rather be drinking beers in the local bar with the rest of his mates. He'd risen to the occasion, though, and made a fond and funny speech, only once making reference to the dire fate, involving a locked room and a shotgun, that would befall Gary if he didn't look after Brittany in the manner to which she'd become accustomed.

Sara stretched her aching legs and flexed her feet to try to ease some of the tightness in her ankles. The heat was a killer. Every cell in her body throbbed with tiredness. She reached across to set the alarm for tomorrow morning – or, rather, later *this* morning;

the clock already showed one forty-seven. She'd been on her feet more or less continuously for – she counted on her fingers – over eighteen hours, and would be up again in five more. But tomorrow would be easier, now that the wedding itself was over; just the Sunday brunch, most of which the caterers would be bringing, and then some of the guests would start to leave, once they'd waved the bride and groom off on their honeymoon. Brittany and Gary would clatter off down the drive, their hire car covered in shaving foam and bedecked with tin cans and inflated condoms, heading for Bordeaux airport and a week on a Thai beach.

She moved her feet again, sliding them on to a cooler patch of the cotton sheet. Having to work in temperatures of thirty degrees or more was draining. When they'd moved here the year before last, Sara and Gavin had sought out the sun, enjoying the novelty of the sensation of heat on their skin as they worked to transform the château into the perfect wedding venue. They'd been so excited: who'd have dreamed that they'd be able to afford this beautiful place? But by scraping together every penny of their combined savings, Gavin's inheritance and the money from the sale of Sara's flat, and by haggling hard on the price, they'd managed it and, miraculously, Château Bellevue de Coulliac was theirs. Next year, at the end of what would hopefully be their second successful season, they'd hold their own fairy-tale wedding in their very own French castle, set among some of the finest vineyards in the world . . .

So, like all the brides she'd seen come and go this summer, Sara should have been fizzing with a sense of joyful anticipation – instead of these feelings of dread, this sense of voiceless suffocation. Not to mention a longing for the comfort of physical affection that had lodged itself under her ribcage like an ache. Of course, it wasn't surprising that Gavin no longer had much time or energy for that side of things; he was working so hard and for such long hours. She tried to remember when they'd last lain together like that, the feeling of his sun-warm skin, his arms, strengthened and tanned a deep mahogany after days spent labouring outdoors, holding her . . .

Maybe things would be different again once they had their first successful season under their belts.

Sara massaged hand cream into her work-roughened hands, easing round her engagement ring, now slightly tight on her heat-swollen finger, and then reached over to switch off the bedside lamp beside her. She'd leave the one on Gavin's side of the bed on, for when he finally made it back to the cottage.

For the wedding season, they'd moved into this basic little stone house, with its one cramped bedroom and single living area with a galley kitchen in one corner, tucked in behind the château next to the walled vegetable garden. At the moment, the walled garden was a jungle of weeds set solid in the heavy clay, which by this stage of the summer had been baked cement-hard, nothing useful growing there other than the ancient, lichen-crusted pear tree in the corner and some herbs that she'd planted up in an old stone trough. But Sara had plans to get to work this coming winter to create a proper *potager* with neat raised beds of fresh produce in time for next year's season.

She'd found an ancient notebook in a tea chest full of old documents when they were clearing out the attic. The leather-bound book was a bit tattered around the edges, but its pages held plans for the layout of the gardens alongside lists of plants. It had taken her a while to decipher the handwriting in places – some sections were rain-blotted or written in faded pencil – and she had the sense that this was a real gardener's journal, used in earnest to establish the gardens at the château over a century ago.

In places, the old structure was still visible, but years of neglect had buried the paths and flower beds under a blanket of stinging nettles and the voracious tendrils of brambles. In the end, they'd resorted to using a digger to clear the ground so she could start all over again with a blank canvas, but she'd been determined to use as much of the original layout as she could, so finding the notebook with its sketched plans was a godsend. It was slowly taking shape, recreating the elegant sweeps of planting that drew the eye through the castle grounds to the views across the river valley beyond.

Gavin had relished driving the digger, carving swathes through the weeds and leaving bare earth in his wake. But that was about as far as his interest in gardening went. She recalled the morning when he'd told her the rest was up to her to sort out and gone off to write a few emails inside. That was one of the first times she'd heard that tiny whisper of doubt.

As she lay waiting for sleep to come, alone with her whirling thoughts, the heat seemed to press in on her from all sides. A faint, sulphurous waft of drains hung in the hot night air, a reminder that the sink in the cottage's tiny bathroom was blocked yet again. Their priority had been to get the guest accommodation perfect in the time available: their own summer digs had had to wait, and so things in the cottage were still pretty basic. She'd need to sort the blocked drain out again tomorrow – another task to add to her already lengthy list.

The disco in the barn, which Gavin had been DJ-ing, had fallen silent about half an hour ago, so hopefully he'd join her in bed soon. As long as he didn't settle down with some of the hardier wedding guests and get stuck into another bottle of whisky. It had happened a few times now. When Sara had questioned the wisdom of this – after all, they had to be up early again the next day and back on duty – he'd just laughed and told her that socialising with the guests was an essential part of the business, good for public relations, it was all part of the job. She'd get up first in the morning to set out a few breakfast things for any early-bird guests and leave Gavin to lie in for a precious extra hour or two of sleep.

She gave a little sigh of relief as she closed her eyes, letting the tiredness seep out of her neck and shoulders, her whirling thoughts beginning to settle.

But then she immediately sighed again, with annoyance this time, as someone tapped on the door of the cottage.

Taking a deep breath, she heaved her tired legs back over the side of the bed and pulled on a dressing gown.

'Gav? Sara? It's me, Brittany.'

Sara opened the door to find the bride, in a skimpy wedding-night negligee of peach satin trimmed with black lace, standing on the doorstep. 'Sorry to disturb you so late, only I saw your light was still on. It's Bitsy, she needed a tinkle so I brought her out for a second but now she's run off. I don't know what's got into her, she never does this at home. Could Gavin come and help me find her?'

'He's not back yet, must still be over at the barn finishing up. Come on, I'll help you look. Don't worry, she won't have gone far.' Sara grabbed a torch from the chest of drawers and tied her dressing gown (white cotton, nothing as exotic as Brittany's) firmly round her waist.

They picked their way carefully along the path and then across the lawn, Sara sweeping the torch beam under the trees and into the shrubbery.

'Bitsy! Here Itsy-Bitsy!' called Brittany.

'Shh, better call quietly.' Sara held a finger to her lips. 'Most people are probably sleeping by now.'

They tiptoed on and then suddenly heard a faint yapping, coming from the swimming-pool area.

'That's her!' Brittany's anxious expression relaxed into one of delight.

'Come on, but quietly still, we don't want her to run off again.'

They crept across the gravel path and Sara eased up the latch on the gate in the railings surrounding the pool.

But as she swept the beam of the torch across the paving, she froze in horror, stopping in her tracks so abruptly that Brittany bumped into her from behind. Because on one of the loungers a couple was lying in a particularly intimate position, bucking and gasping as they reached a climax. The torchlight picked out a discarded champagne bottle lying on its side, the crumpled cerise silk of the maid of honour's gown, and then the merry sparkle of Bitsy's diamante collar. The diminutive dog was busily humping the foot of the man who lay on top of Melanie, a foot clad in a distinctive blue, pink and lavender Sebago shoe. And Sara knew, because he referred to them as his Disco Docksides, that the shoe belonged to Gavin, her very own – and now, all of a sudden, ex – fiancé.

ABOUT THE AUTHOR

Photo © Willow Findlay

Fiona is an acclaimed number one bestselling author whose books have sold over a million copies and been translated into more than twenty languages worldwide. She draws inspiration from the stories of strong women, especially during the years of World War Two, and her meticulous historical research enriches her writing with an evocative sense of time and place.

For more information, to sign up for updates or to get in touch, please visit www.fionavalpy.com.